Pandy spotted Apollo and Phoebus buying small spits of meat from a street vendor. Alcie pointed to Demeter and Ceres dancing with two young sailors. Diana and Artemis were standing on the second-story balcony of a building across the square. Dionysus was sleeping on Bacchus, who was leaning against a column.

"They've shrunk themselves to blend in, I think," Pandy said.

"This isn't good," Alcie squeaked out.

"No, I think it's very good," Pandy said.
"Why would they all be here,
if not to help?"

MYTHIC MISADVENTURES
BY CAROLYN HENNESY

PANDORA
Gets Greedy

BOOK VI

CAROLYN HENNESY

BLOOMSBURY
NEW YORK   LONDON   NEW DELHI   SYDNEY

First published in the United States of America in June 2012
by Bloomsbury Children's Books
Paperback edition published in June 2013
www.bloomsbury.com

For information about permission to reproduce selections from this book, write to
Permissions, Bloomsbury Children's Books,
1385 Broadway, New York, New York 10018

Bloomsbury books may be purchased for business or promotional use. For information on bulk purchases please contact Macmillan Corporate and Premium Sales Department at specialmarkets@macmillan.com

The Library of Congress has cataloged the hardcover edition as follows:
Hennesy, Carolyn.
Pandora gets greedy / by Carolyn Hennesy. — 1st U.S. ed.
            p.   cm.
Summary: Pandy, Alcie, Iole, and Homer travel to Rome to search for another deadly evil—greed—and encounter Julius Caesar, and the Roman gods.
ISBN 978-1-59990-441-2 (hardcover)
1. Pandora (Greek mythology)—Juvenile fiction. [1. Pandora (Greek mythology)—Fiction.
2. Mythology, Greek—Fiction. 3. Gods, Greek—Fiction. 4. Goddesses, Greek—Fiction.
5. Adventure and adventurers—Fiction.] I. Title.
PZ7.H3917Paf 2012   [Fic]—dc23   2011049758

ISBN 978-1-61963-010-9 (paperback)

Typeset by Westchester Book Composition
Printed and bound in the U.S.A. by Thomson-Shore Inc., Dexter, Michigan
2 4 6 8 10 9 7 5 3 1

All papers used by Bloomsbury Publishing, Inc., are natural, recyclable products made from wood grown in well-managed forests. The manufacturing processes conform to the environmental regulations of the country of origin.

For Donald
EGO diligo vos, meus maritus!

And for Zoe Hankett . . .
who makes me want to write.

PANDORA
Gets Greedy

CHAPTER ONE

The Forum

If her mind had any less in it—any fewer thoughts—then she probably wouldn't have actually been able to process that it had become mostly . . . blank. She just had one or two random thoughts left to remind herself that she was really not thinking much at all.

Pandy stood in the hot sun fanning Varinia, wife of Lucius Valerius. Occasionally she exchanged glances with Alcie, who attended to Rufina, the senator's one and only daughter, or, as Alcie privately enjoyed calling her, "Pimple on Hades' Butt." The entire family was seated as comfortably as possible in their very-important-politician section of the massive Forum of Rome, only a few meters away from the seating area of the great Julius Caesar himself.

The Forum, several large fields ringed by official buildings, temples, arches, columns, and obelisks, was the very center and heart of Rome. When she walked through, it reminded Pandy of the Agora back in her beloved Athens, only it was larger and more open. It wasn't so much a marketplace as a gathering place for the entire populace, highborn and low. Today, though, a ring had been erected of sturdy but temporary tiers of wooden benches. Most of the benches held the general public, but some had been sectioned off for the more important families and of these, some, like Caesar's, had been covered with tents or boards to create shade. Lucius Valerius, however, had strangely decided that shade was an expense he didn't want and now Pandy felt her head baking.

A pageant was in progress on the largest field and thousands of spectators, peasants and noblemen alike, were watching the entertainment. A troop of children, having rehearsed for a week, were now presenting a reenactment of Caesar's recent defeat of Pompey, accompanied by acrobats flipping and tumbling in the background. The children waved their toy swords in the air as the child with the honor of playing Caesar, who couldn't have been older than six, pretended to thrust his tiny blade again and again into anyone who happened to be close by, including and mostly his own "troops."

Caesar clapped his hands, throwing his head back in laughter.

"If I had done *that*," he roared, "there would be no one to celebrate with me! No one to share the triumph of the day!"

The crowd around him applauded wildly. Then, when the child "Caesar" got terribly tangled in the blue strips of fabric that represented the Rubicon and fell on his backside, Caesar nearly fell off his golden traveling chair.

"I got wet, indeed," he said, getting to his feet and clutching his sides in glee. "But not *that* wet!"

As she fanned Varinia, the sun making her slightly nauseated, Pandy stared down at the field; yes, it was amusing, but she knew she needed to be thinking about something else. That prospect, however, seemed to overwhelm her; fanning Varinia was boring but simple. So was scrubbing the house floors. So was serving as Lucius Valerius's page and water-girl when the senate was in session. Was she getting lazy? She *couldn't* be . . . she'd put Laziness in the box of great Evils weeks ago! She needed to find Greed! Why in the names of all the great Olympians had she stalled?

She instinctively squared her shoulders. Then she let them sag again, remembering . . .

It wasn't bad enough that she hadn't been able to talk to her father for days; that might be explained by the distance or the hour or whatever her father had been doing at the exact moments she'd called. But the moment Homer had been separated from them, she and Alcie had become so thoroughly depressed, it was as if a lamp had been extinguished in them both. He was there one moment and gone the next. Where did he go? She couldn't ask Lucius, Varinia just shook her head if Pandy broached the subject, and Rufina only smirked. The unfairness of it all was too much. She knew she'd messed up months ago when she took the stupid box to school. Okay, she got it! But she was working like Hercules to make everything right; she was holding up her end and it just seemed like she couldn't catch a break . . . or her breath. She was tired of losing the people she loved. She was tired. Period. She cried herself to sleep every night and slapped herself awake each day. Now, she had no desire to laugh at a stupid, pretend kiddie-war when her quest was nowhere near complete and she was almost past caring.

Alcie, however, began to laugh with the rest of the crowd at the antics below—the first laughter Pandy had seen from her friend in a long time—and that distraction caused Alcie's fanning to slow down considerably.

"Fan faster, slave!" Rufina hissed at Alcie.

"Yes, mistress," Alcie said and began fanning Rufina so fast that she, once or twice, lost control of the heavy rod capped with ostrich plumes and lightly tapped Rufina on the top of her head. Not entirely by accident.

"Daddy!" cried Rufina.

"What is it?" asked Lucius, his eyes scanning the crowd.

"She's beating me with the feathers. Can't I have her executed, pleeeease?"

"We'll see," said Lucius, paying absolutely no attention to his daughter.

"Rufina, stop it," said Varinia. Then she turned her attention to her husband. "Lucius, what are you looking for?"

"Not *what*, good wife," he replied. "*Who.*"

At that moment, a cheer went up from the crowd as "Caesar" began his final assault on "Pompey." Then, as the crowd watched in horror, the poor, confused little boy made the serious mistake of turning and running away when the child "Pompey" came out to meet him in battle. The little Caesar ran straight to his mother, who had been cheering from the side of the field. A hush fell over the crowd at the mere and unintentional hint that the actual Caesar might have shown any cowardice in the real battle. The mother turned ashen and she shooed her son back out onto the field, practically beating him about the ears, but the crying child wouldn't go. Julius Caesar stood as still as any of his many statues that had been hastily erected all over the city, his eyes in slits as he watched . . . his laughter stopped. *All* laughter had stopped. Some of the children stopped waving their swords and looked for their families in the crowd, some sat down on the field, and some ran to tumble with the acrobats.

"Jupiter, protect us all," murmured Varinia.

Suddenly, his mother picked "Caesar" up in her arms and, grabbing his weapon, charged with him back onto the field and straight at the child "Pompey." "Pompey" took one look at the large woman heading straight for him with a short wooden sword and sprinted as fast as his legs would carry him, screaming, into his own mother's arms.

No one, either standing or in the hundreds of seats surrounding the field, moved a muscle. No one breathed. The child would be severely punished, it was certain, but this affront to the new ruler might even call for death. All eyes were on Caesar.

He said nothing for a long time, his gray eyes narrowed and focused on something in the distance. Then he looked down and a smile slowly crept across his face. When he raised his head again he also raised his arms and gestured to take in the entire crowd. Even Pandy's wandering thoughts were brought up short as she stared at the handsome man in the spotless white toga and crown of gold laurel leaves, riveted as to what he would do next.

"I have always said it is the mother that truly makes the man," he shouted. "My mother was with me in spirit that fateful day, urging me on to the greatness and glory you see here before you! It is her victory as much as mine. Well done, boy!"

Shaking with fear, her teeth chattering, the boy's mother held her child up for Caesar and the crowd to see. She took his little hand and waved it to all in the Forum, then she bowed low to Caesar. Clutching her child close, comforting him as he wept with exhaustion, she quickly left the Forum . . . in case Caesar should have a change of heart.

"Wow!" Alcie mouthed to Pandy.

Pandy nodded, her eyes wide. She didn't know of— or couldn't remember—any single person back in Athens with the kind of power that Julius Caesar had. Only Zeus—and maybe Apollo—had such an incredible ego.

The last of the child warriors were ushered from the field as Caesar called for bread and wine to be passed throughout the crowd. Hundreds of slaves appeared with baskets and pitchers, feeding the hungry Romans.

"Does the great Caesar not worry," Lucius called out across his VIP section to the ruler, "that he will deplete the granaries with such a quantity of bread given freely to the unwashed masses?"

"My people will want for nothing," Caesar replied.

"The empire will be founded on many things, not the least of which will be bread and circuses. Full bellies and happy minds, two of the bricks in the foundation, Lucius."

"Got any idea what he just said?" Alcie asked Pandy out of the corner of her mouth.

"Something about going to the circus on a full tummy," Pandy whispered, bowing her head toward Alcie.

"Do they always talk like this?" Alcie asked. "Even in the senate?"

"Especially in the senate," Pandy replied. "They're politicians."

"You two! Silence!" Rufina hissed.

Varinia looked at her husband, not for the first time in the past weeks, with a mixture of disgust and concern.

"Husband," she said softly, "you are known to have the most generous of natures. Why do you care that Caesar gives bread to the crowd?"

"My taxes paid for that grain. I don't want it going to common people. And if Caesar is so free with grain," Lucius said, low enough so as not to be heard, "how will he replenish the silos when they are empty? Perhaps he will tax us all even more! And since he just gives things away, what else of the noble Rome will he give to anyone who asks?"

"Lucius, you are making absolutely no sense!"

"I tell you now, Varinia . . . that man is *not* the ruler Rome needs."

"Hush," Varinia said, panic in her voice.

"You hush," Lucius said. "And stop bothering me. I am trying to find someone."

Pandy had heard her mother and father fight occasionally, but she couldn't conceive of a husband talking to his wife with such disrespect . . . and certainly not in front of others.

Suddenly, she was aware of a low hum all about her as a new excitement began to build in the crowd. Anticipation was growing; something was about to happen on the field below and she was only catching snippets of conversations:

"I've heard he's quite the fighter . . . I guess we'll see, won't we?"

"He's performed splendidly in the practice ring, but that's not to the death, now is it?"

"He's a bit young to be a champion; at least that's what some people say."

"Who's he fighting? Really? Oh, too bad for the boy."

All at once, Lucius stood up and pointed to someone pacing on the side of the field.

"Fight master!" he yelled at the top of his lungs.

A burly man, dressed in heavy fabrics, with many metal cuffs on his arms, turned to stare up at Lucius and gave a slight but respectful nod of his head. Pandy gasped; even at such distance she could see the man's face was streaked with pink and red scars and one eye was gone. He hadn't even bothered to cover it. She turned to share the horrible sight with Alcie, but Alcie was staring straight ahead and Pandy could tell her thoughts were far away.

Alcie, for her part, was thinking about a plateful of roasted dove hearts and how she would give anything— maybe even her own life thread—if she could just spend one rotation of the sundial popping them into Homer's mouth. Just one rotation.

"Oh, Homie," Alcie sighed softly.

"I am warning you now," Lucius said loudly, as Varinia desperately tried to pull him back down into his seat. "He either wins and my wagers are successful, or you will find yourself at the end of my sword!"

"Lucius!" Varinia hissed. "Have you gone *mad*? What is wrong with you to threaten the fight master so?"

The fight master lowered his head, then looked back at Lucius from under heavy eyelids. He knew better than to return the threat, although he could take Lucius in a fight of any kind, without blinking. But Caesar was in attendance and returning a taunt from a silly senator was not going to be tolerated. The fight master bowed low and continued to pace at the side of the field.

"Don't turn your back on me!" Lucius began.

"Lucius Valerius!" came a call. Lucius turned to see Caesar making his way down and over several sections until Caesar was no more than two meters away. "You would kill the poor fight master? He who has trained your would-be champion?"

"Uhhhh . . ."

"What if everyone took on so? We would have no one left to instruct our gladiators."

Pandy jerked her head up. For the last several moments, she had again stopped paying any heed to the events around her in the Forum, ignoring the blustering senator, the hot sun . . . even the imposing new ruler; as Lucius's senate slave, she would be seeing a great deal of him. She had turned her thoughts inward, trying to focus on Greed. She remembered that their first few days in Rome, the three of them—herself, Alcie, and Iole (when they could talk to her)—were spending every moment trying to solve the mystery of where it might be hiding. Pandy had determined that the only time she or any of them could search was at night; they would slip out of the house after everyone had gone to sleep and cover every centimeter of the city. She and Alcie had chosen the following night to begin, and *that* day, a slave girl was brought back to the senator's house and severely punished for sneaking out at night and trying to escape. Pandy couldn't see the punishment herself, but the girl's pitiful cries were enough to keep Pandy and Alcie from venturing out. Pandy fanned Varinia and thought about what else she could possibly do.

And then she heard the word "gladiator."

It was as if a rock hit Pandy in the stomach. With that one word, she knew exactly where Homer had gone over two weeks earlier. She tried to get Alcie's attention, but Alcie was still in her daydream.

"Since I have never known you to be so serious about a wager, especially one over a silly human life," Caesar went on, "and since I have no idea what you might do to others should you owe them money, *and* you know I cannot afford to have you murder the entire senate *just* at the moment . . ."

Caesar looked at the crowd and waited for the polite laughter at his joke to die away.

". . . And since Caesar finds himself in a gracious and generous mood this day, I shall assume responsibility for all wagers you have made. If your fighter is victorious, Caesar himself shall pay you. If he is not, Caesar will pay your debts and the fight master will retain his head. Is that acceptable to all?"

Several voices, those who had bets with Lucius, all called out in agreement.

"Yes," Lucius said finally, looking down at Varinia, who had her head in her hands, utterly humiliated. "Caesar is very generous."

"That I am," Caesar said, returning to his seat. Then he turned toward the field and motioned to the fight master. "Begin!"

From the far end of the Forum, a double line of soldiers marched onto the field. In between them walked two figures in full gladiator dress. One man carried a whip and a shield. The other, a tall blond boy, carried a shield and a sword. Pandy's heart flipped over.

Then, from way across the Forum, high on the roof of the Regia, Rome's first royal palace, a glint of metal caught her eye.

There it was again.

Was somebody signaling something? To her? To someone in the Forum? She looked around at the crowd. Everyone she saw was staring at the procession of the guards and the fighters; no one but her, it seemed, was watching the Regia.

Just then, in silhouette, Pandy saw two figures—men, she was certain—standing atop the building. One was standing with his arms crossed, but the other was fidgeting with a large shield, sunlight bouncing off the metal. Almost at once, there was a familiarity to these two; Pandy was certain she knew them . . . but how?

She squinted; sometimes narrowing her eyes caused blurry faraway objects to become clearer. At first, she thought both men were bald, but Pandy then realized that both were wearing helmets—and black breastplates—and had huge shields. They appeared identical in every way.

"Helmet? Black breastpla . . . ?" she murmured. "Ares? *Ares?* And . . . ?"

Then, from far away, she heard the echo of both men laughing at the same time and saw one slap the other on the back. Then the slappee slapped the first man back . . . harder. The first man then threw a punch, which knocked the second over and out of sight. But he was back up in an instant and landed a blow to the other man's midsection. Suddenly, the fight became so fierce that, as Pandy watched, they both knocked each other off the roof.

Pandy's mouth dropped, but there was no more time to think about what she'd just seen; a trumpet call brought her attention back to the field and the blond-haired youth.

"More wine, slave," Rufina ordered Alcie.

Alice, still in her reverie, turned to get the wine pitcher from a small bench. A shout went up from the crowd; already they were hungry for the spectacle, the skill . . . and the blood.

"Alcie!" Pandy said, this time loud enough to shake Alcie from her dream.

"What?"

In that instant, Pandy couldn't decide whether to tell her friend to look or not look; either way, Alcie was going to have to turn around sometime.

"*What?*" she mouthed again.

Pandy tilted her head and Alcie, holding the pitcher, turned and followed Pandy's gaze.

Then she lost her grip on the handle and gasped, spilling the wine on Rufina's head.

"HOMIE!"

Within a heartbeat Rufina leapt up and struck Alcie across the face. Varinia was on her feet immediately and caught her daughter's hand before it could deliver another blow. Although by that time Alcie had balled up her fists and was ready to give as good as she got.

"Sit down!" Varinia said.

"She did it on purpose!"

"I am terribly sorry, mistress," Alcie said to Varinia, unclenching her hands and not even looking at Rufina. "It slipped. It won't happen again."

By then, the soldiers on the field had formed a large ring around the two opponents and Homer and the other man were standing, facing each other and waiting for the signal. Alcie, even though she didn't want to give Rufina the satisfaction, glanced at the field.

"Why did it slip, slave?" Rufina smirked, watching Alcie's face. "Did something startle you? Did you see something surprising?"

"Nope. Not at all," Alcie said, mustering every ounce of calm that she could. "May I get you some more wine?"

"No. Just fan me!"

Pandy moved in closer, fanning Varinia with her left hand and holding onto Alcie with her right. Alcie was holding Pandy's hand so tightly, Pandy thought her finger bones might be crushed. Every once in a while, Pandy coughed slightly when Alcie was so terrified by the action on the field that she let her fan stop and Rufina began to tense. But then Pandy herself became riveted.

Homer was wearing arm, shoulder, and shin guards along with a breastplate and a loincloth covered by a short cloth skirt. His opponent also wore the guards, loincloth, and fighting skirt, but his shoulders and chest were bare. Pandy—and everyone else—stared in horror at the dozens of scars, gashes, holes, and bruises covering this man's upper body. Why wasn't he bandaged? Why didn't he hide them away? Then, with a start, she realized exactly why: he was using his mangled, scabbed, and bloody body as yet another weapon to instill fear and revulsion in everyone who saw him—but especially in Homer. And from the look on Homer's face, it was working perfectly.

The scarred man was the first to charge across the field, heading straight for Homer. Homer looked like he'd been dazed or shocked. He was motionless except for his head, which swiveled on his neck taking in the enormous crowd with wide eyes, as the man raced for him and readied his whip. At the last moment, Homer's head cleared and he quickly dodged to the left, but not fast enough. The tip of the whip caught his ankle and Homer went sprawling onto the field.

Alcie shuddered and gripped Pandy's hand tighter. Rufina giggled.

Homer was on his feet fast, but not before the man snapped his whip again and slashed Homer's calf.

"Callus! Callus!" the crowd screamed in praise of the other man's skill.

Pandy felt her heart sink even further. This man, Callus, was too good, she thought. Clearly *he* did not drop out of gladiator school with a desire to be anything else—like a poet. This man was a warrior and would be until the day he died . . . which was probably not going to be today.

Homer felt the flesh tear away from his lower leg and stumbled back but stayed standing as the crowd booed and cheered. He and Callus circled each other for some moments, then Callus charged again. This time, however, Homer was ready. He saw the angle of the whip as it whistled through the air and raised his sword, succeeding in batting away its stinging tip. A great cheer went up from certain areas, catcalls and shouts from others.

"Excellent move, boy!" called one man.

"It was luck and nothing more," countered another.

On the field, Homer heard the cheers and felt slightly better about his chances. He'd hated Whip Basics back at school, but he remembered enough that he thought he might just be successful. Then Callus sent his weapon low and took Homer's legs out from under him a second time. As Homer fell, Callus rushed in, seeing his chance. He sent his whip through the air again, but this time, from the ground, Homer raised his sword and caught the end, winding it around the blade. He jerked his sword quickly, yanking the whip out of Callus's hands. Homer got to his feet and ran, cutting off his opponent, as Callus tried to retrieve his whip. Unable to get to it, Callus simply charged, yelling with all his might, right at Homer's shield. It was a daring move. Callus had no weapon and was trying to beat Homer down into the ground.

And then Homer found his strength. He was actually slightly larger than Callus and he fought back with both his sword and shield. Slowly, he drove Callus across the field, careful to steer clear of the whip lying on the ground, as the crowd rose to its feet and screamed itself hoarse. Homer's drive was deliberate and he could sense that Callus was beginning to tire. Then, Callus switched his shield to his other hand. Homer, unprepared for this move, sent his sword slashing into the open air. Callus dropped to his knees and smashed his shield into Homer's wounded leg. Homer cried out and fell backward. Now, Callus towered over him. Homer defended himself against Callus's shield as best he could and once succeeded in grazing Callus on his arm. But after several long agonizing moments, Callus knocked Homer's sword out of his hand and raced to pick it up. With his shield and Homer's sword, Callus quickly disarmed Homer, sending his shield spinning like a discus through the air, narrowly missing several guards standing off to the side.

Pandy glanced at Alcie and saw a single tear coursing down her cheek, her mouth hanging open. Rufina clapped her hands wildly, and Pandy became so angry that she momentarily lost control of her power over fire, and the next moment, Rufina fainted from a rush of heat washing over her body and turning her beet red. Nobody noticed. Everyone was too rapt by the scene on the field.

Callus stood over Homer as he lay on his back. He pointed Homer's own sword toward his neck and slowly began to pierce Homer's flesh with the tip. He stared at Homer with the steely gaze of a gladiator whose victory was complete.

"He's had it!" shouted some in the crowd.

"Let him go!"

"Iugula!"

Furious, Lucius Valerius was on his feet, his hands clenched at his sides, his face nearly as red as his daughter's, who was now slumped where she sat. Varinia saw her husband's face.

"Why do you fret, Lucius?" she said calmly, her tone only hinting at her disgust. "Remember, mighty Caesar will pay your debts. You will lose nothing if this young man loses his life."

Then . . .

Callus took the blade away from Homer's neck, brought it swiftly up in front of his face, and bowed in salute to Homer. Then Callus turned toward Julius Caesar and brought his sword to his side.

Alcie stood stock-still, but a small moan escaped her lips. Pandy realized that Alcie had a good idea of what was happening, and so did she. In their weeks with Homer, he'd taught them a great deal about what it meant to be a fighter in the ring.

The crowd also knew. The battle had been relatively short, but incredibly fierce. With this one action, Callus was letting everyone know that he respected Homer, his bravery, and his skill, and he was asking Caesar to spare Homer's life.

All eyes turned toward the man with the golden wreath on his brow, and Caesar, in turn, cast his eyes over the crowd. What did *they* want? Did they want to see this young man perish? His mind spun: he wanted to give his people their desire, but, with his reputation for bloodthirsty victories, he wanted to show a more generous side to his nature—at least in the first few moons of his rule. Fortunately, what Caesar saw most was compassion for the youth on the field. Many in the crowd were showing their approval for mercy by pressing their thumbs and forefingers together—the *pollicem premere*. Caesar didn't necessarily have to turn his thumb up or down to signify death. All Caesar had to do was turn his thumb at all. Even the tiniest bit.

Caesar raised his hand high for all to see. Pandy and Alcie held their breath.

Then . . . ever so slightly, Caesar pressed his forefinger into his thumb.

Pandy let out a terrific whoop as she felt Alcie slump against her, sobbing. The crowd went wild as Callus tossed the sword to one side and began to walk off the field. Then he turned and, extending his hand, helped Homer to his feet. This sent the crowd into a deafening fit of good cheer; bread was thrown onto the field and many people danced in their seats. Rufina woke up and demanded to be fanned but Varinia shushed her.

"But I'm hot!" Rufina whined.

"It's all over and we'll be home soon enough. Pandora and Alcestis, clean up now. No one is going to fan anyone."

Suddenly, Varinia was aware that Lucius was standing beside her—not moving. She stood and followed his gaze. He was staring straight at Julius Caesar. Moments later, there was a small lull in the roar of the crowd and that was all Lucius needed.

"Mighty Caesar!" Lucius bellowed.

"Lucius!" Varinia cried, clutching his robe. "What in the name of Mars are you doing now?"

"Mighty Caesar," Lucius called out again, shaking Varinia's hand from his toga. The crowd between them quieted as more and more people began to look from Lucius to Caesar and back again.

"What is it you wish, friend?" Caesar said, a tiny frown creasing his brow for only an instant.

"Your mercy is great."

"Indeed," Caesar said. "But I believe it was the will of the citizens."

Those who could hear murmured in assent.

"Yes, the youth would have been killed had it not been for the citizens," Lucius said, as Varinia stood by, her eyes wide. "But you alone had the power to spare him and he lives. My champion lives! Is that not some sort of victory for me? Will Caesar not pay his debt to me?"

"*Lucius!*" Varinia spat.

"You cannot be serious, Senator," Caesar said.

"I am."

The crowd began to mutter among itself. They were used to spectacle, but not from their chosen leaders who attempted to demonstrate only noble and dignified behavior.

"Then you have been in the sun too long, my friend," Caesar said after a pause. "Your champion lost and I am paying off your wagers with others, is this not enough? Do you want more, even if it were to defy logic?"

"I merely wish you to render unto me that which is mine."

Caesar was dumbfounded and stared hard at Lucius.

"Very well," he said finally.

Shock ran through the crowd, which began to openly dissent; voices were raised in anger and disagreement. The citizens of Rome were proud of one thing, above all: their collective ability to understand what was logical. This dispute was not.

"Bring the youth to me!" Caesar called.

"Gods," Alcie mumbled to Pandy. "He's gonna do something to Homer! This is so not good."

In the time it took Varinia to explain to her husband that his family was about to become a laughingstock, Homer was led up through the tiers of seats and made to kneel in front of the ruler. Caesar looked at Homer, his face devoid of expression. When he looked at Lucius again, his face was unreadable.

"I shall pay you, Lucius, as well as your losses," Caesar said. Then he raised his voice for the entire Forum to hear. "And I thank you, honorable Lucius Valerius, for your gift to me of this worthy champion! He will be a prized addition to my household. And, once his wound is healed, perhaps we shall wager again the next time you send a warrior into the ring . . . whenever you obtain another warrior, that is. Perhaps I shall even bring him as my attendant to the feast you will hold. In your home. In my honor. Mere days from now."

Lucius's face turned violet, but Varinia stepped in front of her husband before he could speak.

"Thank you, Caesar. Your generosity—and patience— are a blessing upon us all."

With that, Varinia yanked on Lucius's robes with such force that he was nearly knocked over—which caused some of the crowd to twitter.

"Rufina, help me get your father out of the Forum," Varinia whispered as she led Lucius away.

Moving slowly to follow the senator, Alcie and Pandy both tried to get Homer's attention as he was raised to his feet. Pandy watched as Caesar gave some instructions to a nearby attendant without ever taking his eyes off Lucius.

"Whadhesay . . . whadhesay? Pandy? Did you catch it?" Alcie asked.

"Something about stables. I think I saw the word 'stables,'" Pandy answered.

"I just know I'll never see him again," Alcie moaned.

"Alcie, stop it," Pandy said, handing her the fans as she gathered the wineskins and Lucius's water pitcher. "Five ticks of the sundial ago, we thought he was dead. Now, we know where he's going. We might not be able to get to him, but we know he's alive!"

CHAPTER TWO
A Darkened Room

"You like?"

"Oh, yeah," Hermes replied, surveying the tiny room. The dim light from the single rusted torch cast large shadows as he surveyed the cracked, nearly crumbling walls, the water seeping onto the dirt floor from unseen sources, and the rank, fetid smell. "Yeah! It's disgusting. It reminds me of her. Perfect-o."

"Not too small?"

"Not at all," Hermes said, shaking his head, then gazing up at the ceiling, which looked like it might cave in at any moment. "Now if she were together—reassembled, you know—then we might have a problem. But the pieces will fit quite nicely in here. This room makes me think of her brain: tiny and empty. And that long corridor we took to get here . . . that's her heart. Dark and cold."

Mercury shook his head and set against a wall the beautifully wrapped package he'd been carrying.

"How can you talk about her like this, Brother?" he said. "Aren't you worried about the consequences she might deliver? You could end up as a block of marble at the bottom of the ocean or as a lump of granite in a hill on some faraway island. And where, I might ask, would that leave me? What would I do with no counterpart? Did you ever think of that, huh? The balance of things would shift tremendously all over the known world. What if she were to find out about all these yowza oh-no-he-didn't! things you've been saying?"

"First off, it's not just me who's talking, it's everyone who's ever *met* her and you know that. And how would she find out? How could that possibly happen?" Hermes asked, his eyebrows waggling and a grin spreading out over his perfect face. "Her head is still in Persia! Her glorious, empty head is still under the transformation spell that turned it into a pair of red leather sandals, which I was graciously allowed to stuff under a couch in the home of Douban the Physician . . . the new Douban . . . the young man that Pandora likes so much. It will only be when I carry Hera's head, which includes her big ears, over the Persian border that the enchantment will lose effect and her enormous mouth will start yapping and her brain will start thinking her ugly thoughts. We can speak freely, Brother; the peacock can't scream just yet; Hera has no idea what is happening at the moment."

Hermes casually tossed his package alongside the other.

"Plus, Zeus would never permit her to harm me; he's having too much fun watching what Pandora does to his wife, whether or not he would ever admit it."

"Jupiter is enjoying it as well," said Mercury. "So, what do we have? I mean, which parts of her are here and what's still back in Persia?"

Hermes looked at the packages.

"Well, as you know Hera was transformed into five pairs of walking sandals with extra cushiony comfort . . . easy to do because she's so gargantuan . . . to get Pandora and her friends across the Arabian desert."

"I know this indeed," said Mercury.

Hermes walked to one wall and, with a great flourish, swiped his arm in front of it. Immediately, the gray wall seemed to dissolve and a scene appeared before both gods. It was Pandy's last moments in Persia.

Immediately, the spell was broken.
Pandy and Douban quickly turned to look at
Alcie and Homer, both having stepped over

the Syrian border, both now barefoot. In front of Alcie, lying in the sand, was Hera's right leg complete with one golden sandal. Lying at Homer's feet was Hera's left arm, her rings and bracelets glinting in the sunlight.

No one spoke for a long, long time.

Then Pandy had an idea.

"Iole and Douban, please remove your sandals," she said, taking off her red leather footwear. Then, with her hands, she dug a shallow pit and buried all three pairs.

"Pandy!" cried Iole.

"Well, what do you suggest?" Pandy cried desperately. "We can't have her following us!"

"No, you can't," said a familiar voice. "At least not for a while."

"Ah," said Mercury. "And *that's* where you came in and whisked them here to Rome!"

"Right. Alcestis and Homer actually reversed the transformation on their particular pairs of sandals by bringing them out of Persia, so here we have a leg and an arm. The other leg and arm, in sandal form, are safely hidden in a tiny little border town and Hera's head and torso are, as I said, in Douban's home—hopefully being peed on by the family dogs."

"But Pandora and her pals have been here in Rome now for almost three weeks!" Mercury said. "Why have you waited until now to bring the pieces together?"

Hermes stopped and slowly turned to look at Mercury, his almost exact double in every way right down to the winged sandals and helmet. He stared at the same perfect face—only now *that* face had a silly, questioning expression—and hoped against hope that *he* would never be that dumb.

"Okay, I'm gonna let you think about what you just said for a tick or two."

"Whaaa . . . ?"

"*Why* didn't I bring Hera here sooner? Why didn't Zeus want me to reassemble the demon so she could terrorize Pandora a little bit more?"

"Stupid question?" asked Mercury.

"Why does *everyone* want me to wait until the last possible moment to piece together the cow? Knowing that when she's fully formed and fulsome in a blue robe there will quite probably be Hades on earth? That Pandora possibly—no, probably—no, definitely *won't* finish her quest? That when Hera assumes ultimate power, not only will she decimate Pandora and her friends, but she'll begin to ruminate on exactly how she'll punish all of the rest of us for the assistance we gave Pandora here and now? That I will be so very, very lucky if I only end up at the bottom of the ocean?"

"Stupid question."

"*Why* does Zeus want his wife back only when absolutely necessary?"

"I give! I give . . . ," Mercury said, laughing.

"You bet you do! Watch what Hera did after she murdered Alcie in Aphrodite's own temple," Hermes said, swiping his arm in front of the wall again. The scene playing out was Hera and Aphrodite in Aphrodisias.

When the last flames were out, Hera instantly turned on Pandy, her chest heaving and her arms raised again, and found Aphrodite standing in her way.

"Move!" she commanded.

"I'm sorry," Aphrodite said sweetly to the smoldering, hairless goddess with the blackened robes. "Come again? I didn't quite catch that. Certainly you would not be giving me any orders in my temple, would you?"

"Aphrodite, get out of my way!"

"Why? One little girl a day isn't enough for you? All I see is you having a rather bad hair day. You know, I could fashion a wig for

you. Would you like that? Borrow some of Demeter's leaves . . . or just put a sheep on top of your head?"

"I still can't believe Aphrodite actually *insulted* Hera while she prevented her from killing Pandora in Aphrodisias," Hermes said, watching the scene go dark.

"Aphrodite is lucky Zeus has been just a little more involved in this whole mess lately. But for that alone, Aphro will be fortunate if she's only turned into an oil lamp. Why, indeed! Such a no-go, Bro."

"But how does Zeus or Jupiter, or whoever, know that this is the last possible moment? I have been having so much fun . . . *not* . . . with all my Greek relatives visiting here in Rome that I just haven't been thinking too much about Pandora and the exact reason that everyone has made the trip. Jupiter has had me flying all over the place, dropping off welcome baskets and heated Roman bath towels, delivering messages and the like. Busy, busy."

Mercury stepped to the wall and waved his arm. Instantly, Hermes saw everything that Mercury had been doing.

Aphrodite deciding that she wanted a dark-haired slave boy for her foot massage while

Venus emphatically insisted on having a blond. . . . Mercury nodding furiously.

Mars demanding a sparring partner well versed in the broadsword at the same time Ares demanded a knife fight.

"It never matters what they use, they just end up trying to kill each other," Mercury said as the scene shifted again.

Athena, in the food-preparation room, trying to talk to Mercury about Plato when Minerva walked in and started talking about Cicero. Then both goddesses turning on Mercury, saying that they actually wanted to talk to Cicero.

"And I have to *find* the poor man, wake him up." Mercury sighed. "It's endless. It's hard enough being messenger to my immortal Roman brothers and sisters; now I have to handle our Greek doubles! Two goddesses of the harvest, of the hunt, of wisdom, et cetera. Two gods of wine, of healing, of the oceans, blah, blah, bleck. So you probably know more than I do at this point, even though you've been having an easy time of it; off eating spiced lamb and other exotic eastern delights, making sure no one digs up a few pairs of sandals."

"I know, I know, pal, and I'm grateful you've been handling the menial parts of 'our' job," Hermes said. "Zeus wanted to get everybody off Olympus for a bit; change of scenery, it's true. But the Greek contingent is really here to help if it's necessary. Zeus and Jupiter aren't certain what's going on, they just know that she's been here exactly nineteen days. As per Zeus and Jupiter's instructions, I placed Pandora and pals in the home of Lucius Valerius . . ."

"He's a senator," Mercury cut in. "And a good one from what I am told. Generous, smart. Nice-looking wife."

"Yes," Hermes continued, "well, smart he may be, but it didn't take much to cast a spell over his entire household to make everyone think that Pandora, Alcestis, and Homer had been house slaves for years. They fit in quite nicely at first."

"At first," said Mercury, waving his hand:

> A well-fed Roman maiden was making eyes at Homer directly in front of Alcie and Pandy.
>
> "Do you not find me attractive, slave boy? Me, Rufina, a senator's daughter?"
>
> Homer began to turn red and gag slightly.

"You Romans and your Roman ways," Hermes said. "Sheesh! Even the maidens!"

"It's the same in Greece!"

"But we're much more civilized about it—about everything. Do you ever watch your worshippers? How far they take everything? The excess? And how much they *eat*! And *then* what they do?"

Mercury looked hurt, Hermes recognized it at once.

"I don't think it's necessary to disparage our entire general populace. I know we have some bad eggs here and there, but we're doing all right for hovering on the verge of being *the greatest empire in the known world*, thank you very much!"

Hermes laughed.

"One of 'em anyway. So Rufina takes one look at Homer and decides he's the oatie cake she wants on her plate. But then, when she saw how Homer and Alcie looked at each other, she convinced her father to . . ."

"Right, right!" Mercury interrupted, waving on the scene:

> *Lucius Valerius, a gray-haired man of imposing stature, was handing Homer over to several men in the dead of night. Rufina was standing at the top of a staircase, a giant smirk on her face.*

"Do I have your word you will make a champion out of him?" Lucius said. "I may safely wager on him as my prized warrior?"

"You have our word, Senator!" one man replied. "Or he'll be dead within the week."

"Then I'll want my money back!" barked Lucius.

"Right!" Hermes cut in. "So that's where Homer is now. Pandora and Alcie have no idea where he's gone and have been out of their minds with worry and work."

"And they don't see Iole very often because she's become a . . ."

"Vestal Virgin," Hermes said. "I was completely unprepared for that. I miscalculated when I materialized them all into the household and Iole ended up in the . . . what do you call it?"

"I just call it the Vestal's room," Mercury said.

"Well, with the spell of familiarity on the entire house she became the Vestal, junior class, no questions asked. You know, we have priestesses back home in Greece, and they're important—very sacred. But they don't seem to have quite the importance that yours do here in Rome."

"Oh, you bet!" said Mercury. "Vestals are tops! If they happen to be walking about on the streets, they can pardon, on the spot, someone condemned to death and on his way to be lion food. But you'd better not touch 'em. Bad news. What about the dog?"

"Dido was protected under the same spell as the girls. Lucius's wife, Varinia, loves him; thinks he's been their pet for years. He's on a long tether in the back garden and she sends out the best of the table scraps after every meal. Pandora is with him as often as possible."

"So," Mercury said. "She's got five evils in the box; pretty close to the end of her quest."

"Yeah, but this one seems to have her stumped. And to make matters worse, she can't concentrate on it because of all the preparations she and Alcestis have to help with for the big celebration."

"Well, it's not every day Rome gets a new ruler," Mercury added. "Big doings. And Julius Caesar's no ordinary mortal. He started what amounted to a civil war in these parts and then, completely defying logic and all his advisors, he took his troops across the river Rubicon and beat the togas off Pompey and his men, basically destroying a treaty that said Caesar, Pompey, and some other general would split everything three ways. Done and done. Then he just crowned himself ruler of Rome and on and on and on."

"I like him," Hermes said thoughtfully.

"Me too."

"He's a doer. He gets things done."

"Gotta respect."

"Gotta."

"So," Mercury went on, "a week ago, Caesar declared the start of a period of celebration and heavy-duty feasting which will conclude with a really big blowout in a few days at the home of Valerius. All of Rome is buzzing with who's going to be invited, what to wear, and some such nonsense."

"That's gonna be some bill!" Hermes snorted.

"I wouldn't want to pay it."

"And that, my brother from another mother, is why Zeus wants me to start bringing the Hera parts to Rome. He and Jupiter have decided that *all* the immortals are going to the final feast."

"So then, Pandora has nothing regarding . . . ?"

"Greed? Nope, not yet. She's been scrubbing floors and washing Rufina's hair, gabbing with Alcie and sometimes Iole. Everybody got caught up on various adventures in the underworld and Persia, they kidded Pandora about the young boy, Douban, who likes her so much, and all of them put their heads together about where Greed might be hiding. At night, she told everything to her wolfskin diary, and then, one day Pandora tried to call her father back in Athens on her shell . . ."

"Oh no!" Mercury said.

"Oh yes," Hermes replied.

"But doesn't Pandora know that they've all traveled . . . ?"

"No, of course she doesn't know. None of them know. Why would they? I haven't told her what happened when I brought her here. My orders were to get her settled and am-scray. And I haven't seen her since. And, these kids have never seen Rome before. And it hasn't changed that much in . . ."

"Well . . . not so's you'd notice anyway," Mercury assented.

"And when she couldn't talk to her father, she became so depressed. Then Homer was sent away and Pandora just had the wind slowly knocked out of her, day by day. Now, she's basically ignoring the whole reason she's here. Everyone has noticed. Ares said, offhandedly, that he thinks she's given up. Athena got so mad at him, she turned his head into a boil and popped it with a meat spit."

"Why don't you at least tell her about her father and the . . . ?" Mercury began.

"Because Zeus thinks it shouldn't be that big a deal. Prometheus is one man and, as far as Zeus is concerned, Pandora is fighting to save all of mankind."

"You know Pandora almost better than anyone," Mercury said. "What do you think?"

Hermes was silent for a moment.

"I don't think she's given up, but she's definitely lost focus. And she's depressed; she's almost too discouraged to even panic."

"She's tired," Mercury said.

"I know. But if she thought it was bad before, I cannot imagine how she's fared at the Forum."

"Oh, right . . . the entire household has gone to the Forum to see the . . ."

"Right," Hermes agreed.

"It's probably gotten worse," Mercury said.

"Much."

CHAPTER THREE

Iole

In her tiny, windowless room—a closet hastily but unquestioningly converted into sleeping quarters when she appeared in the household—Iole sat in front of the small looking glass. In the light of the single candle, she carefully dipped the large, soft brush in the pot of colored powder and dabbed at her cheeks. Without warning, the brush slipped out of her grasp and left a reddish streak across her chin. As she fumbled for a cloth to wipe it away, she knocked over a pot of silver powder and watched it settle onto her ceremonial robe. She wiped the red streak off her face then stood and carefully shook out her garments. Sitting down again, she dipped a smaller brush in a pot of black kohl paste and tried to line her eyelids, but only succeeded in looking like the wrestlers back at the Apollo Youth Academy in Athens when they got punched in the eye. Again she tried wiping it away, but only smeared it all over her face along with the red powder already on the cloth. Iole wiped her hands, deciding to let the black paste dry a bit, and dipped her forefinger into a little tub of red goo. She smeared it on her mouth, then smacked her lips together. When she smiled, most of the goo slid off her lips and onto her teeth.

"Gods," she said, wiping her teeth with the cloth and turning them black. "This is simply not the avocation for me."

"Iole!" came a call from the corridor. "They'll be here any moment. Are you ready to go?"

Melania sailed into the cramped room and Iole caught the woman's dim reflection in the glass. She was dressed in white from head to toe, her golden hair done up with combs, pins, and veils, and her face painted so heavily but so beautifully that she could have rivaled Aphrodite. And Melania had something even the great Aphrodite didn't have: a sound to her movements. Whenever she walked, there was a slight tinkle, as if tiny bells were ringing off somewhere.

Melania, the head Vestal Virgin assigned to the house of Lucius Valerius, was the closest thing to physical perfection in a human that Iole had ever seen, and that included Pandy's mother, Sybilline—who was pretty perfect. The only thing that marred Melania's perfection now was the hint of a scowl that crossed her face when she looked at Iole. She stood in the doorway and stretched out her arms, as if she were helpless against an onslaught of frustration. Iole was completely spellbound by this stunning creature, as if she had come up on a doe in the forest and just wanted to stare for hours. In fact, as far as Iole was concerned, Melania was even *more* beautiful than Aphrodite or her Roman counterpart, Venus.

"Let me guess. You don't like being the junior Vestal in the Valerius household and you have decided to run away and join the theatre? No? You're going to entertain the grotesque populace between gladiator fights? No? Oh, I *know*: you're joining the circus!"

Iole just slumped where she sat.

"I can't seem to get the hang of it," she said softly. "All these pots and brushes. I don't know which to use for what. Also . . . I am finding it rather arduous to see in the dark. Perhaps another candle? Just a bit more light . . . ?"

"Nonsense! I have taught you everything you need to know to adorn yourself even if your eyes were plucked from their sockets!"

Iole was horrified. The Romans, she had learned in her few weeks among them, seemed to tend toward the bloody and brutal before they thought of anything else. Athenians, she remembered with a pang of homesickness, were of a loftier mindset whereas these people, even the supposedly high-minded VVs, were just . . . gory.

"You have an undeveloped but innate ability," Melania went on. "You simply lack any real creativity—or form—or desire, I'm guessing. That's fine I suppose. There are Vestals who wear no makeup to be sure . . . although no one likes to be around them. Or pardoned by them. Or counseled or prayed for by them. Look at you, Iole. You are a beautiful maiden. At least, you are underneath all that paint. Why do you think you were chosen from among most young girls to take on this responsibility? To attend the College of the Vestals? Which is your household of origin, again? I can't seem to remember."

"Uhhhh," Iole hesitated.

"Well, it doesn't really matter. The point is that you were chosen not only for your innocence and purity, but for your extreme good looks . . . as was I. As were we all. At least . . . I think you were. I have been known to be wrong. Not often. At any rate, let's clean you up."

At that moment, they both heard a chorus of voices raised in song, carried toward the house on a light breeze.

"Ah . . . they're here!" Melania said. "Good. I'd like

them to take a look at you; perhaps tell me where I am going wrong. Come along!"

Moving down the corridor from the back of the large house to the front, she called down to two slaves, bidding them to open the large wooden doors and then, with Iole at her side, Melania again stretched her arms wide as twenty or so women entered from the street. Most were wearing white, but some of the younger ones, the junior VVs like Iole, were clad in shades of gray.

"Sisters!" Melania sang down to them, stretching her arms out even further. Iole didn't know if this was tradition or if Melania simply enjoyed stretching. It did give almost anyone who was close to her the impression that Melania not only knew exactly what she was talking about at any moment, but that she was also extremely . . . grand . . . and oh-so worthy of respect.

"Sister!" the group called up, almost in unison.

"Have we a moment?"

"We do," answered a slightly older woman. "We received word that the battles in the Forum have concluded, but the crowd is still filing out of their seats. We may actually have several moments before we must join the procession to the Theatre of Pompey in celebration of Julie. What do you wish?"

"Julie?" thought Iole. "Who's Julie?"

"I wish a bit of older counsel with the young one here," Melania said, as all eyes turned to Iole, who suddenly wanted to drop through the floor. "She does not understand some of our ways and I don't seem to be able to get through. She also, obviously, has trouble looking pretty. We need a Vestal intervention!"

Almost as one, the group headed up the stairs. Iole thought for a moment that they looked like an arc of doves or a flight of swans.

Then all at once, she felt a different pair of eyes on her; someone staring—the way no one else ever had. And it wasn't the first time she'd sensed it since she'd been in the house of Valerius. She'd never been able to locate the source, but now she looked all over and finally caught sight of the large front doors and one of the slaves now pushing them shut.

Crispus.

The handsome youth with the curly black hair was staring back up at her even as he threw the heavy bolt into place. When he saw her catch his eye, he immediately diverted his gaze; he knew what it would mean for both of them if he was caught looking at the pretty Vestal. Death.

Iole was beyond confused. Even her mighty, mighty brain had never anticipated this. She simply assumed that she would be alone for the rest of her life. She'd go into a science, if she could; perhaps become the first female physician or astronomer or something of that sort. But this . . . this was an instantaneous shock to her system. Someone was looking at her the way Homer looked at Alcie. The way young Douban had looked at Pandy! This wasn't part of the plan! This wasn't supposed to happen to . . .

She suddenly started to cough. She found herself, inexplicably, unable to breathe. And she couldn't walk, at least she didn't think she could. Her legs were stiff as wood. Is this what attraction meant: utter loss of motor skills? Complete inability to do *anything*? No one had told her any of this, no one had prepared her; not her mother, nor Pandy, nor Alcie. And they were supposed to be her best friends . . . well, Pandy, anyway. She never *did* trust Alcie . . . and he was still *looking* at her!

The women crowded around Iole, blocking her view of Crispus, each one giving little tidbits of information about what it meant to be a Vestal.

They began with things Iole already knew: maintain the sacred fire in the Temple of Vesta, bake the sacred salt cakes to be used for the many ceremonies, dedicate oneself to the rites and rituals of Vesta for thirty years. . . .

Iole began to say, politely, that she already knew all of this.

Then the advice veered toward the slightly odd.

"When you pardon a condemned man on the street, don't look him in the eye," said one woman. "You don't want him to get the wrong impression. You're saving his life, Sister, not being friendly."

"That's right," answered someone from the crowd.

"Uh-huh!"

Iole saw that all the women were starting to get very worked up, very excited by the conversation.

"But we are compassionate, correct?" Iole asked.

"Right," said another. "But superior."

"Superior!"

"And, when you get your salary from the state treasury," said a third woman who was so thoroughly draped in fabric that Iole wasn't certain how the woman could lift her own head, "don't thank the treasurer. After all, it's the least we're due—not being able to marry for thirty years or have children and all."

"All right," said Iole, thinking that was a bit haughty.

"However, you *are* allowed to not only thank the new ruler and look at him directly, but you may call him by his pet name: Julie," said Melania. "If no one else is around."

"Huh?" said Iole, taken aback.

"Tell it, Horatia!" Melania called to a junior VV standing at the back. "Let's see how much of the story you know."

"Let's see!" said another Vestal.

"Well," said Horatia, pushing her way to the front of the group—which by this time had maneuvered Iole back to her small room and, taking up every centimeter of available space, had somehow managed to sit her down at the dressing table. "Not so long ago there was a man named Sulla . . ."

"*What* was his name?" asked the group.

"Lucius Cornelius Sulla," said Horatia. "The Senate drew up a list of everyone who Sulla thought was an enemy of the Roman Republic. And if the Sulla didn't like you, you were on the list. And then Sulla was given the job of carrying out the proscription."

"Proscription!"

"Which meant that it was his job to condemn you and see to it that you were executed."

"Harsh!"

"*Harsh!*"

"Well, one day Julius Caesar's name appeared on that list."

"On the list."

"Little boy!"

"Hail Caesar!"

"And he was condemned to death. But the Vestals found out about it and interceded on his behalf."

"Put a stop to it!"

"The man's alive to-*day*!"

"And that is why the Vestals may look Caesar in the eye," said Horatia.

"Call him 'Julie.'"

"Because," Horatia finished up, "we saved his life and he knows it! He's ruler, but he knows which side of his bread has the honey."

Without warning, as Iole was listening and looking, Horatia moved slightly to the right and Iole caught a fleeting glimpse of two identical faces at the back of the group . . . incredibly beautiful faces. She nearly gasped as the two women winked at her in unison. Then Horatia shifted again, and the women seemed to vanish.

"Excellent, Horatia! And thank you," said Melania. "All right, sisters, what we really need now—because *tempus fugit*—are your best makeover tips."

"Oh, and will you just look at this child?" said the woman with the heavy headdress, tilting Iole's face upward for everyone to see the black and red streaks. "I thought she was going to run away and join the circus."

The next instant, as Iole was trying to remember where she had seen those fleeting faces before, her face was wiped clean and there were more than several hands drawing and dabbing, painting and polishing her skin. And there were so many beauty secrets flying into her ears, Iole thought she might go deaf.

"White lead and white chalk . . . white complexion."

"Charcoal for bad breath."

"Soot on the lashes and brows. And give yourself one nice long brow. Very pretty."

Every once in a while, a question or comment concerning Iole from one woman to another would break through.

"Do you think she was really the prettiest in her family?"

"I know you have to be mentally fit to join the VV priestess-hood, but she can't seem to grasp any beauty basics. I'm not sure she's all that smart."

Iole craned her head around to pinpoint exactly who it was who'd questioned her intelligence. But then, all their voices began to blend into one cacophonous drone and Iole tried desperately to suppress a giggling fit. She was trying to listen to these women and their ideas but it was being crowded out by the image she was concocting in her mind. She again pictured the group as they had marched up the stairs as one single unit. Then she found herself imagining the Vestals as a pack of lovely and gentle but wild animals allowed to run free in a meadow somewhere. They were tall, shapely, pure white (like Dido), impossibly silly yet magnificent. She imagined them moving as one: something would spook them and they would run this way or that, stopping at watering holes, eating leaves off trees and jabbering like crazy birds the entire while. What would they be called, she wondered? A passel? A flock? A herd?

She also found herself being extremely touched by the amount of time and attention they were paying her. They truly wanted her to succeed at being pretty. They didn't particularly know or care that she was smarter than any five of them put together; their concern was for her outward appearance, but in a way that was almost sacred. The Vestals represented something higher and finer, and their beauty was a . . . a . . . connection to that nobility. Again, she realized that no one had ever taken this kind of care or time with her before. Not her mother, but then, she was just a little girl when she'd left home so many weeks earlier. Not Pandy . . . well, she was trying to capture all the evils in the world; she had other things on her mind. But Alcie could have given her a few tips!

"And last but not least," said Melania, shooing the others away as she moved in gently, a brush in her hand tipped with something red. At that moment, Iole felt an enormous warmth and gratitude toward the older woman as she realized that there was a part of her, down very, very deep that secretly enjoyed being beautiful and being *made to be* beautiful.

"Crocodile dung for the cheeks!"

Iole froze in horror as Melania brushed her face with the sticky substance.

"A little red ocher, wine dregs, and mulberry juice mixed in for good measure but the real trick is crocodile dung! And now, my dear, you are ready to go out in publicus."

The passel of Vestals—Iole had decided the word was "passel"—headed back down the stairs and out once more into the street, carrying Iole along as she tried in vain to catch any scent of dung from her face. There was nothing offensive and Iole prayed that at least the dung had been dried before it was mixed with anything else.

As they walked along, pardoning condemned men and offering up the quick prayer here and there, the group was joined by Vestals from other parts of Rome until there were, Iole thought, perhaps as many as fifty beautiful women strolling the streets. When they came upon the throng moving toward the Theatre of Pompey, the common folk parted and allowed the Vestals their own spot in the procession, which the Vestals assumed with great dignity—and Iole followed suit—spreading their arms high and wide.

CHAPTER FOUR

Insula, Sweet Insula

The series of apartments that Jupiter and Zeus had created for all the gods to inhabit during the Greek gods' visit to Rome was as large as a temple. There were four floors, each with many rooms all decorated according to the tastes of the individual immortals. Artemis's and Diana's rooms were similar in their collection of hunting bows. Dionysus and Bacchus each had a wine press and a grape arbor hanging from the ceiling. Apollo and Phoebus Apollo had an extensive medical library and walls hung with dozens of musical instruments. Persephone and Proserpine had each plastered on their walls at least five full-size posters of Hades and Pluto, covered with hundreds of berry-juice kisses. And so on. There was also an enormous roof garden, indoor bathing pool and archery range, and, although no immortal actually *had* to cook, a huge food-preparation room.

Athena and Minerva, determined to be wise and knowl-edgable about all subjects, had decided to prepare all the meals while in Rome—the mortal way—as long as the other gods took turns doing the dishes.

"I am only saying that I'm not sure it is the wisest course of action," Athena said, deeply inhaling the steam rising out of the cooking pot. "Oh my, but that smells delicious!"

"Wait till you taste it!" Minerva replied. "Now, regard-ing today; normally, as you know, I would agree with you wholeheartedly. But if it's one thing I'm sure of, it's Rome. The populace has been seeing our pairings, albeit sporadically, for days now. I don't think anyone will be too alarmed at seeing all of us at once."

"Zeus and Jupiter are determined that we all attend this celebration today and I am convinced that more than a few of your citizens will faint from a . . . a . . . deity overload. Did you say five peppercorns?"

"Five, that's right," said Minerva.

"Pass them to me will you, dear?"

"Look at it this way," Minerva said, handing Athena the small jar of black, green, and red corns. "If we all bunch together, most people will think we're some sort of theater troupe, painted up to look like gods. But if we spread out a little, I think most won't notice."

"I hope you're right," sighed Athena, putting the lid

on the pot to catch the steam. "I wonder what Pandora will think when she sees us. We've all been so careful to stay out of her sight. Zeus really wants us all to be strictly a safety net; he wants her to do this all on her own. But from what Hermes has said, she's lost her way."

"Well, seeing all of us today—with no Hera in sight—just might be the boost she needs, Gray Eyes," Hermes said, popping his head into the enormous food-preparation room. "Sorry, make that Gray Eyes times two. Hello, Minerva."

"Hermes."

"And you never know," he continued. "Pandora is one of the most unusual maidens I have ever met. Spirit, guts, courage . . . I have to believe this is a temporary slump. You two almost ready to go?"

"We've just come from scouting and the procession is in full swing!" Mercury joined in, his head just above Hermes'.

"We only need to season this," Minerva said.

"What are we having?" Dionysus asked, tottering in from the hall.

"Baked dormice," Athena answered, without turning from the cooking pot.

"Love it!" sang Bacchus, skipping past Dionysus, a wine bottle in his hand.

"You'll love it later, Uncle," said Minerva. "It's for the

evening meal. Excuse me, but is that Venus's magic girdle in your hand?"

"Uncle Dio," Athena said, turning her head to look at Dionysus. "Why is Aphrodite's undergown on the top of your head?"

"Welllllllll," Dionysus answered, pulling off the gown and waving it like a scarf. "It happened like this . . ."

"We wanted to have a little impromptu music session with Phoebus and Apollo," Bacchus cut in. "But Ceres and Demeter had turned their ankles on the stairs and the golden boys were debating about the best way to heal the ladies. So then we thought we'd trim our hooves, y'know, make a good showing since we're all going out soon . . ."

"But Ares and Mars were fighting over who got to use the lavatorium next," Dionysus took over. "So we, Brother and I, just *happened* to wander up to the roof of the insula and who should we *happen* to spy but Aphrodite and Venus. They had just come back from checking in on that little maiden. One of Pandora's friends . . ."

"The smart one," Bacchus interrupted.

". . . right, the smart one. And they were sorta lying around . . . sorta . . ."

"Sunbathing!" Bacchus giggled.

"And we just wanted to make certain that they get a nice tan," Dionysus went on.

"A nice allover tan!" Bacchus said, doubling up with laughter and nearly falling on the floor. "And if they don't have anything to cover up with . . ."

"You *stole* their clothes?" Minerva asked.

"Okay," said Hermes, turning for the stairs. "Well, Mercury and I gotta run!"

"Stay right where you are!" barked Athena. "You two are not going up to the roof. Dionysus, Bacchus, give Minerva and me their clothes and girdles right now; *we* will take them up as soon as I finish seasoning this dish. Honestly, the nerve!"

"I wouldn't blame them if they turned you two into drunken raccoons after you stole their things," Minerva agreed, taking the goddesses' clothing, placing it on a chair, and turning back to the cooking pot. "Now, Sister, which wine to use? Diluted or undiluted?"

"I say undiluted," Athena said, turning to the storage shelves and reaching for the bottle. "Where's the wine?"

"I hear someone calling," Bacchus said, tearing out of the room. "Don't you, Brother?"

"Huh?" said Dionysus. "Oh! Oh, yes! Coming, Zeus!"

"They've stolen the wine!" Minerva cried.

"I'm going to turn them into raccoons myself. Father *isn't* calling you, you overgrown Satyr!" Athena said, tossing her wooden spoon onto the counter. "Now give me that wine!"

Both gods fled on their goat hooves to the upper levels of the insula as Athena and Minerva tore after them, trying in vain to grab the wine bottles from their hands.

Hermes and Mercury tiptoed over to the cooking pot and Mercury was about to lift the lid.

"Don't touch that!" yelled Minerva from the stairwell.

Mercury yanked his arm back.

"How do they always know?" he whispered.

Just then, there was a shriek from the stairwell and Aphrodite and Venus ran into the food-preparation area, completely unclothed with only their long, golden hair covering everything that needed it, followed by Bacchus and Dionysus.

"Do you have our clothes?!" Venus shouted.

"Gosh," said Hermes, all innocence. "They were around here somewhere."

"There!" shouted Venus, pointing to the chair.

"We just want to say we're sorry!" pleaded Dionysus, he and Bacchus racing after the goddesses as they dashed away, hurriedly flinging on their garments.

"How about a hug?" called Bacchus.

There was a long moment of silence as Mercury and Hermes just stared at the spot where Venus and Aphrodite had been only moments before.

"I think that may have been worth the entire trip," Hermes said, slowly.

"Even if Pandora doesn't succeed," agreed Mercury, still rapt.

"Pandora? What's a Pandora?"

Athena and Minerva bolted back into the kitchen. Hermes and Mercury simultaneously pointed in the direction everyone had run off.

"How did they get *by* us?" Athena said, sprinting with Minerva close behind.

Suddenly there were two loud thuds.

"OW!"

"Sorry," Hermes heard Minerva—or was it Athena— say. "We're after the wine."

Diana and Artemis stumbled into the kitchen, each one rubbing her shoulder.

"Everyone has completely lost their minds!" Artemis said. "They're running around like a spooked herd of sacred cows!"

"Zeus and Dad are getting ticked off. They want to leave already. Now, *we* are ready to go," said Diana to Mercury. "You?"

"Ready," said Mercury.

"*Stop sneaking up on me!*" Juno screamed from an upper floor.

"It's like she's here in the room," Artemis said quietly.

"It's a voice that carries, certainly," agreed Hermes, flicking a piece of lint off his toga.

"*And stop shooting arrows at me, you little gorgons!*" they all heard Juno shout.

"Cupid and Eros still trying to make her fall in love with the furniture?" asked Diana.

"*I will take those arrows and give you both such a . . .*"

"Looks that way," said Mercury.

No one said anything for a long time, but everyone was trying to imagine Juno gazing lovingly at a couch or a chair or a floor rug.

"Dinner smells good," said Artemis after a moment.

"Sure does," said Diana.

At that instant, a puffed-up blowfish sailed into the room and stuck in Diana's elaborate hairdo.

"I've got a fish on my head, don't I?" she asked calmly.

"I would have to say . . . yes," Mercury said.

"A little help? Wanna just send that back this way?" came a call from the large front room. The two messenger gods and the two goddesses of the hunt strolled out of the food-preparation room.

"Over here?" said Poseidon, waving his arms and splashing about in his traveling tank. "Right here? Thanks! Right here?"

"Here, please?" said Neptune, splashing Poseidon with his tail. "Right here. Thanks so much."

"Oh, you bet I'll give this back," scoffed Diana as she

began to climb the stairs to the second level. "Artemis, will you help me get the fish out of my hair?"

"Absolutely."

"C'mon!" said Poseidon. "We're playing puffer-toss and I'm up three to one!"

"Only because you cheat!" argued Neptune.

Suddenly, there was a blinding flash and Zeus and Jupiter were standing in the middle of the room. They listened for only a moment to the commotion going on all over the insula. As they both turned to look at each other, they clapped their hands once simultaneously and, after another brilliant flash, all the immortals, Greek and Roman, stood before them, impeccably dressed.

"We have had just about enough of all of you," said Jupiter.

"We have given you all free reign to do, see, mingle, and roam about as you please," Zeus went on. "Now Jupiter and I wanted to see this new ruler among his people; this Julius Caesar who will become so powerful and do so much for Rome. We asked only that you be ready to attend one tiny little celebration and you ingrates can't even manage to do that."

"What do you have to say for your miserable selves?" Jupiter spat.

"Sorry," someone said from the corner of the room.

"I'm sorry."

"We're sorry."

"Uncle Dio stole the wine . . ."

"Do you still have the wine?" Dionysus whispered to Bacchus.

"No wine," said Zeus.

"*We* were ready!" sang out Artemis and Diana.

"Kiss ups!" someone whispered.

"Stop!" Zeus said.

"We're off!" Jupiter said.

"Wait!" Minerva cried.

Everyone watched as she and Athena waved their hands toward the food-preparation room. Then the goddesses turned forward again.

"Had to put out the fire under the dormice," Athena said, as if everyone should have already known that.

"Away!" said Jupiter and Zeus together.

The next moment, the large room was completely empty; only a single wine bottle remained, rolling lazily in the middle of the floor.

CHAPTER FIVE

The Theatre of Pompey

The throng in front of the Theatre of Pompey (one of the few monuments built by Pompey that Julius Caesar had allowed to remain after their battle) was so thick that Pandy and Alcie had climbed onto the second tier of an enormous marble fountain to get a better view and avoid being crushed. From there, Pandy was able to assess just how tightly the crowd was jammed in.

The square in front of the curved theatre was actually large, but almost all of Rome was in attendance so it appeared quite small.

"That is some wild building," Alcie said, looking at the front facade: a huge, three-tiered, perfect semi-circle of arches. "Although I'm not really feelin' why Caesar decided this was the best place to slam together thousands of people."

"You should see it inside," Pandy said. "Get this . . .

it's all based on our amphitheaters back home in Greece. The Romans sorta stole our idea, but instead of building into a hillside for support, they figured out a way to put this whole building on its own foundation. And, there aren't supposed to be any permanent structures for plays or speeches or things like that inside the city walls, because the Senate doesn't want the people being ... how did one senator put it? Oh yeah, 'being whipped into madness.' So Pompey got around that here by adding a temple dedicated to Venus, I think, at the very back. Now it's big-time sacred and stuff. Clever, huh?"

Alcie was just staring at her.

"And you know all this ... how?"

"This is where the Senate meets."

"And puts on plays?"

"Gods! No, falafel-brain. The Theatre of Pompey is where the Roman Senate meets for now."

"Oh, *this* is where you and the senator work? *This* is where you go every day?"

"He works. I get him water."

"That's work."

"This building is just a temporary thing until their regular building is redone. That place, the regular one, *was* called the Curio Cornelia ... after the last ruler, Cornelius, or something. Julius Caesar is having it completely rebuilt and named after him, so the whole

Senate has to meet here until the Curio Julia is finished."

"Hermes' toenails," Alcie said, dropping her voice. "Caesar's got an ego the size of the Parthenon. Hey! Maybe it's a lesser evil we can capture: ginormous ego!"

"I think we took care of that when we put Vanity in the box. But from what I've seen, it's different with this guy. I hear some of the senators talk about Caesar before he became ruler; when he was leading the Roman army all over someplace called Gaul. How he was right down in the middle of the battles with his men. And everyone could tell that it was him because he was the only one wearing purple. They say both armies could see this purple speck flying from one battle to another, wherever the fighting was worst. So his men had a lot of respect for Caesar because he was hacking and slashing right alongside them. And, of course, they won. Caesar seems to really care about Rome and the people; he just wants to leave his mark, y'know?"

"I still think tearing down a perfectly good building just to put up another perfectly good building is dumb."

Rufina, seeing that two house slaves, one of whom she happened to despise, had a better vantage point than she did, insisted that she wanted to stand on the platform instead and kept hitting Alcie's legs in an effort to knock her off. At one point, Alcie kicked Rufina—not hard, but hard enough.

"Mother!"

"What is it?" Varinia said absently, paying no attention to her daughter.

"That wretched slave kicked me in the head!"

"Hmmm?" said Varinia, turning her gaze from the crowd and surveying the situation.

"I want to stand up there and I want *that* one put to death!" Rufina cried, pointing to Alcie.

Alcie pretended to be absolutely engrossed with the scene around them and looked around innocently.

"Blessed Minerva!" Varinia said. "Stop it, Rufina! Just stop it! I am sick to death of your complaining about that girl. As if I don't have enough to worry about with your father these days. And you cannot stand up there; it would be unseemly for someone of your status to allow people to stare at your feet, wondering about the shape of your legs and such. Children and slaves, fine; but not you."

Alcie grinned at Pandy, then stuck her tongue out at Rufina, who glanced up just in time to see it. Rufina said nothing, but her face became very serious before she looked away.

"You've done it now," whispered Pandy with a smile.

"Yeah," Alcie said. "Oogly-boogly. I'm so scared."

All at once, Pandy saw two figures on top of the Theatre of Pompey: the same two men she'd seen earlier on the roof of the Regia. It was Ares and Mars, she was certain.

"Gods!"

"What?" Alcie asked.

"No . . . Gods!" Pandy gasped. "Alce . . . look!"

But Alcie had spotted something else.

"No, *you* look!"

Pandy followed Alcie's finger as she, trying to be inconspicuous, pointed into the crowd. In the middle of the crush of people, Pandy clearly saw Athena. Then she saw a woman standing right next to Athena who looked like she could be Athena's twin. Neither of them wore their helmets nor carried their shields, but Pandy had seen Athena many times; she even carried a small carved bust of the goddess that would offer advice if Pandy got into real trouble. She knew the severe features of Athena's face. That meant the other one had to be . . .

"Minerva!" Pandy whispered.

"No way!"

"Way," Pandy said. "*And*, I think that's Ares and Mars on the roof over there."

"What are *they* doing *here*?" Alcie asked. "Is this good or bad, good or bad?"

"I don't know."

Suddenly, a blend of melodies and harmonies floated over the crowd, signaling the approach of the Vestal Virgins. Amazingly, the crowd parted, crushing everyone further, allowing the band of women to climb a short set of wooden steps onto a large dais set up in front of the theater. Pandy and Alcie forgot the immortals for a moment as they watched the line of sacred woman, their voices raised in song, moving gracefully up the stairs.

"I don't see Iole," Pandy said, straining her eyes.

"You don't suppose they left her at the senator's house because she can't sing, do you?"

Before Pandy could answer, Alcie gripped her arm.

"Wait! I think I . . . ," Alcie said. "I . . . no . . . you've got to be kidding. I see her!"

"Where?" Pandy asked, looking intently at the group of Vestals, Junior Class bringing up the rear.

"Second row, third from the left," Alcie answered.

Pandy stared for a long moment.

"No way!"

"Way!"

"She's . . . she's got makeup on," Pandy said. "And her *hair*! She's . . . beautiful!"

"Our little girl is all grown up," Alcie said solemnly, then she started giggling.

Suddenly, Pandy gave a start.

"Aphrodite!" she all but squealed.

"Aphrodite's what? What?"

"There."

Without warning, two other women, nearly identical in every way, had joined on to the very back of the Vestal procession. One woman was singing in time with the others; the second woman, Pandy could tell, didn't really know the words and was a beat behind everyone else.

"Venus and Aphrodite," Pandy said, remembering every aspect of Aphrodite's face. Aphrodite had held her so close when Pandy had sobbed over Alcie's death, there was no way Pandy would ever forget anything about her.

Then, Aphrodite turned and winked at Pandy. Pandy nearly toppled off the fountain. Aphrodite nudged Venus, who also turned, still singing, and gave a little wave to Pandy and Alcie.

"Wave back," Pandy said, recovering herself. Alcie just stood slack-jawed. Finally, Pandy picked up Alcie's hand and shook it for her. Then Pandy spotted Apollo and Phoebus buying small spits of meat from a street vendor. Alcie pointed to Demeter and Ceres dancing with two young sailors. Diana and Artemis were standing on the second-story balcony of a building across the square. Dionysus was sleeping on Bacchus, who was leaning against a column.

"They've shrunk themselves to blend in, I think," Pandy said.

"This isn't good," Alcie squeaked out.

"No, I think it's very good," Pandy said. "Why would they all be here, if not to help?"

"To watch us all die horrible deaths?"

Suddenly, a thought hit Pandy like a bolt of lightning.

"Where's Hera . . . and Juno?"

Before Alcie could even try to come up with an answer, someone was shoved into Lucius, who crashed into his wife, who crashed into someone else, sending a ripple effect throughout the crowd.

"Jupiter," Lucius said loudly, straightening himself and his wife. "If Caesar doesn't finish the Curio Julia soon, I'll . . ."

"You will what, noble Lucius?" came a question from close by.

Lucius snapped his head and found himself almost face to face with Julius Caesar, on his way to the dais, who had stopped when he heard Lucius's comment. Lucius realized that he, and everyone else, had been pushed out of the way to make room for Caesar's entourage.

"Please go on," Caesar said with a smile that wasn't really a smile. "If I don't finish the Curio soon, you will . . . *what*?"

"I will . . . continue to serve Rome and its citizens in any and every way possible," he said. "And from whatever location Caesar decides, be it the Theatrum Pompeium or the Curio Julia, should it ever be completed, or the top of a tree."

"The top of a tree!" Caesar laughed. "Perhaps that can be arranged, Senator. I should like to see you legislate from amongst the leaves!"

Those closest to Caesar laughed as Lucius fought to keep from turning red with anger and humiliation. Caesar's entourage continued forward until at last Caesar mounted the dais and turned to face the crowd.

"Citizens of Rome!" he began, and from the time it took the sun to move from three to four on the nearest sundial, Caesar saluted the populace, told of the glories that were in the city's future and detailed the far reach of the Roman Empire. He made clear that Rome was and would continue to be, "until the moment Phoebus refuses to pull the sun across the sky," the greatest city in the known world.

"Athens," Alcie coughed in disgust, covering her mouth.

Fortunately no one had heard except Pandy, and Pandy dug her fingernails into Alcie's wrist when she saw Alcie was about to say it again. Caesar went on to tell how he was going to urge the Senate to allow the building of permanent structures for sporting games, chariot races and theatrical productions.

"I envision a Colosseum, a hippodrome, a Circus Maximus. And I believe that you, the people of Rome, will *not* be incited to riot at the sight of the spectacles of skill and daring to be held in these places. We witnessed such a spectacle today . . ."

At this, he motioned into the crowd and Homer, flanked by two men, walked nervously onto the dais.

". . . and you did not tear down the scaffolding at the sight of the mercy shown to this noble youth! I believe, and the Senate will know, that you are above such behavior!"

The crowd cheered loudly. It was Alcie's turn to grip Pandy at the sight of Homer.

"Easy," she said to Alcie. "Easy, we can't get to him yet."

Pandy looked about, seeing senators she knew shaking their heads slightly and pursing their lips in subtle disagreement at Caesar's edict.

"I shall also, as one of my first acts, declare that one of our immortals—someone who deserves a higher place in the pantheon of the gods—be given her rightful status!"

The crowd hushed.

"I shall completely redesign, rebuild, and reroute

the sewer system and, at various points, erect temples to one of our most important but often overlooked deities: Cloacina, Goddess of the Sewers!"

At this, the crowd nearly did riot—with joy. Rome had an advanced sewer system, but of late it had fallen into disrepair—which was evident if one took a deep breath.

"I only hope that I live long enough to see the completion of such wonders."

"Hail Caesar!"

"Long live Caesar!"

"You, the citizens of this great Empire," he continued, smiling at the adulation, "may well ask how shall we accomplish these undertakings. How, because we are a generous people, shall we spread this great culture—our knowledge, our wisdom, our art, and our perfect government—from land to land? Well, one way is to conquer anyone who might oppose us and claim the land in the name of ROME!"

The crowd went wild.

"For, as I have shown, no one may defeat our armies!"

Again, the crowd cheered madly. Caesar smiled and held out his hands, signaling for quiet. Then he gave another signal and a second young man was escorted onto the dais.

"But then, we must keep it," he said. "And to that end, I have created . . ."

As if he were a conjurer, Caesar held his hand up high, his fingers closed tight around something small.

". . . this!"

With amazing dexterity, he tossed a shiny object into the air and caught it with only his thumb and forefinger. It was a single gold coin.

"I give you . . . the aureus. This will be the coin of the realm and will from this day forth always bear the likeness of your ruler. Since the gods above have seen fit to bestow that title upon this humble servant, let us hope it is my profile which graces this simple golden disc for many years to come."

"Hail Caesar!"

All of a sudden, Pandy saw Lucius Valerius's head stretch a little longer on his neck. He craned his head over the crown, his eyes focused like a hawk's on the coin. He was much, *much* more than merely interested. In that moment, something buried deep within her—something she hadn't experienced or even thought of in many days—began to bubble.

Her curiosity.

Her insatiable curiosity was boiling up and telling her that something was happening. Something she'd seen for a while but had been too distracted to pay any attention to: Lucius Valerius was obsessively concerned with this gold coin. Could it be the source of Greed?

Perhaps even Greed itself? Caesar had been discussing the size, weight, and purity of the aureus for days with his most private counselors in the Senate; Lucius had been one of them, until he violently disagreed on some point or other and had been excused from further conversations in the "inner circle." She'd been there when, having been dismissed, he'd sat down in disgrace and ordered her to fetch more water. But, her curiosity questioned, why was he the only one possessed? She couldn't remember anyone else being affected to such an extent. Did it have something, anything to do with the Theatre of Pompey? His seat, perhaps? No, no that was silly.

"I wish to acknowledge the artist who has so deftly engraved my Roman nose for all to see," Caesar said loudly, motioning for the new youth on the dais to step to his side. "His very name means creativity. I give you Varius!"

Varius, a pale young man with hunched shoulders who was obviously unused to such attention, looked like he was going to wither on the spot. Caesar gently moved him away and Varius was returned to the crowd.

"Okay, now *he's* cute!" Alcie whispered.

"What are you talking about?" asked Pandy. "He looked like he was going to faint. He's white as a sheet. Besides, you have Homer!"

"First of all," Alcie said, turning up her nose, "he's an

artist! And you have to be very . . . artsy to be an artist, and that includes staying inside a lot. Ergo, no sun. But he's so intense and brooding, I love it! And second, I will never give up Homer. But just because I'm not buying doesn't mean I can't look in the market stalls."

"I think that's what my mother used to say to my father," Pandy said.

"The first minting of this coin will happen only a few days from now," Caesar continued. "As a gift to the people of Rome, I shall give each citizen of the Empire a single aureus. And to my loyal senators, you shall each receive a bag of ten coins at the feast held at the home of Lucius Valerius! Now, let us have music and dancing! Let the celebration continue!"

At once, music filled the air and many people began to dance right in the middle of the square. Others filed off to smaller celebrations around the city, but the space in front of the Theatre of Pompey remained quite crowded as senators grouped together to discuss the day's events and the future of Rome with this new and unpredictable leader.

"Pandora!" Lucius yelled.

Immediately, Pandora and Alcie scrambled off the fountain.

"Master?" Pandy said, approaching quickly.

"Water," he said roughly.

Pandy put her hand on the pitcher hanging from her waist.

"At once," she said, then turned to Varinia. "May I take Alcie with me? She can part a crowd better than I can and I'm carrying the pitcher."

"Very well," said Varinia.

Weaving their way through the crush of people, Alcie nearly bumped into a fountain of drinking water as she tried to keep up with Pandy, who was doing a wonderful job of parting the crowd.

"Hey, Pandy!" Alcie called. "What's wrong with *this* water?"

"Come on!" Pandy yelled over her shoulder.

Alcie grabbed on to the back of Pandy's toga to keep from losing her and didn't let go until they were behind the dais and standing in front of the main entrance to the Theatre of Pompey.

"Are we gonna find Homer?" Alcie asked, excitedly.

"No," answered Pandy, walking up to a large guard. "Besides, you know we'd never get to him and he's probably already been taken back to Caesar's residence."

"Then why are we here?"

"I just want to check something out," Pandy replied, then she looked at the guard. "Senate business."

"You're no senator," snapped the guard with a laugh.

"I am the page to Lucius Valerius," Pandy said,

flashing the seal of the house of Valerius painted on the pitcher. "I enter on his business."

The guard knew better than to argue and stepped aside.

Pandy and Alcie walked through the main arch and portico. After wending their way through a series of tunnels built into the foundation, they emerged into the open air and Alcie turned to see the enormous, empty amphitheater surrounding her.

"Gods!"

"Wild, isn't it?" Pandy said, on the move. "I don't think there's anything this big back in Athens. Lucius sits over here. Y'know, I'm actually kinda surprised there's no one else around. I am so used to senators whispering in little groups or hurrying to their places as Caesar sits on the stage, surrounded by guards and fawning yes-men. Reminds me of how all the girls who wanted to be popular used to stand around Helen and Hippia back in middle school."

"You mean, before they got turned into big black lizards?"

"Yeah, before that," Pandy said, remembering what had happened when the two prettiest and meanest girls in her entire school had asked to see the box of evil just as Pandy was about to take it home. And that's how this whole mess started.

"What are you looking for?" Alcie asked, as Pandy stopped at a specific seat on a long row.

"I don't know, Alce. I just know that the senator is super interested in the new coin. It's pure gold, and if gold isn't a reason to get greedy, then I don't know what is."

Pandy started poking around Lucius's Senate seat.

"But it would affect everyone, wouldn't it?" Alcie asked. "I mean if it's the gold, and we've seen it, wouldn't *we* be hurtin' on each other to get it?"

"Maybe. But it seems to really get to the senator. So maybe it has something to with when he's here."

She stopped and sat down.

"There's nothing suspicious." Pandy sighed. "Nothing even curious. But I had to give it a shot. I'll tell you, Alce, the main thing is I feel like . . . like . . . *myself* again. Gods! I think I'll try calling my dad again later tonight. I mean, he's gotta pick up his shell sometime, right?"

"You know it," Alcie said.

"Oh!" Pandy said with a smile. "I don't know what did it, but two ticks of the sundial ago I was lost. And now, looking at Lucius looking at that coin, it's like I suddenly woke up! We've got two evils left to get and one of 'em is here and we're running out of time."

"What we're really running out of is time to get that water back to Grumpius Maximus," Alcie said.

"There's a fountain for the speakers and performers at the back of the stage," Pandy said. "It's the one I use when the Senate meets. Come on."

Pandy led Alcie up onto the stage and around to the back stairs; they found themselves behind the main theater in a beautiful and well-cared-for garden surrounded by long arcades on either side.

"See that wall way back there and those steps in the middle?" Pandy asked, filling the water pitcher from a bubbling fountain. "Behind it is where Pompey put the secret temple to Venus; almost no one is allowed there."

Pandy put the lid on tight and looked around for Alcie who, Pandy realized, had fallen completely silent. She was standing at the railing of the platform they were on, gazing out into the trees and at the manicured plants, and at the lawns, completely devoid of people. The only sounds were made by birds singing in the trees.

"This may be the most beautiful place I have ever seen," Alcie whispered. "I just want to find Homie and stay here."

"Yeah," Pandy said. "I know, I know. Let's go."

But as they turned toward the amphitheater, a voice—like the trilling of a songbird, only much louder— came like a shot across the garden.

"Alcie, honey? Wait!"

Alcie froze in her tracks.

"Huh?" she said softly.

"Wait, Alcie! Wait! Come on, Proserpine! Don't look at me like that. You've been *wanting* to meet them for days, we finally track them both down and now you're stopping to adjust a *sash*? Well, what then? Oh, your *garland* . . . well, pardon me. Come on, they're right over here. What? I *know*!"

Alcie and Pandy both slowly turned around again and peered into the garden.

"Who is it?" Pandy asked.

"Gaahhhh," Alcie gurgled.

Pandy truly couldn't tell if Alcie was delighted or terrified. Flying across the lawn, spinning their way through the trees, came two identical, beautiful creatures in deep gray robes shot throughout with streaks of scarlet, light rose, and fuchsia. They raced up the stairs and onto the platform; as one girl made a slight adjustment to the garland of spring flowers on her head, the other girl made straight for Alcie, catching her up in the biggest, tightest hug.

"HI!"

"HI!" Alcie managed to cough out in exactly the same tone, although the look on her face was pure surprise.

"Didn't expect to see me so soon, did you?"

"No . . . ," Alcie wheezed. "I . . . I . . . you gotta put me down, please."

"Oh, sorry! Forgot my own strength!" said the girl as she released Alcie. "I know, I *know*! Soooo . . . hi! So much to tell you, but first things first. This is Proserpine! She's me, only Roman."

"HI!" said the first girl, her garland still not quite right.

"HI!" Alcie answered back in a way that Pandy would have scoffed at back at school. So silly, so . . . girly. But now, watching these three, it seemed as natural as rain.

"Now you introduce *your* friend," Persephone said. "As if we didn't already know!"

"I know!" said Proserpine.

"I *know*!"

Alcie turned to Pandy and the most fantastical grin spread over her face. Pandy saw that Alcie was nearly electrified with happiness and strangely relaxed at the same time.

"Pandy—oh, Gods—Pandora Atheneus Andromaeche Helena, this is Persephone and Proserpine."

"HI!!!!" they said together.

From out of nowhere, her mouth opened and . . .

"HI!" Pandy giggled, and she flew into Persephone's arms for her own tight hug.

"Oh, Pandy! Can I call you that? Of course I can! *We* can! I have heard the most wonderful things about you and I have been telling Sistah-Goddess Proserpine here all about your quest and the amazing places you've gone and about Mother's best friend, the she-dog . . ."

"Your Hera, my Juno," whispered Proserpine conspiratorially.

". . . that's right, *our* she-dog, sending Alce here into the underworld and all the fun we had until Buster—Hades—sent you back up topside. And now, we're here! And what's a few years between visits, huh?"

Persephone turned to Pandy.

"Did she tell you all about the underworld? Did she, huh? Huh?"

"She did!" Pandy said, caught up in the excitement, completely forgetting that Lucius Valerius was waiting for his water. "She talked mostly about the food."

"I know! Oh! OH! I nearly forgot," Persephone cried. She pulled a small sack from the folds of her robe. Inside were several clay jars, their lids sealed tight.

"Let's see, what did Cyrene send you? I think there's snail custard, wilted field greens, and maybe, just a few . . ."

"Don't tease. Don't tease me!" Alcie said, stamping her foot.

"Would I do that to you?" Persephone laughed. "Of course she sent a special batch of roasted dove hearts!"

"Now it's a festivaaaaaal!" Alcie squealed.

"But you have to share," Proserpine said.

"As if!"

"You'd better!" Pandy giggled, playfully hitting Alcie on the arm. Then she looked around and shook her head, trying to clear it. Who *was* she? Why was she talking like this? And there was something bizarre Persephone had just said.

"How did you know I was here," Alcie said. "I mean right here, right now? I could have been anywhere!"

"Okay, alpha," said Persephone, "we're goddesses . . ."

"Duh!" said Pandy, parroting what had been Alcie's favorite word on their quest.

". . . so we can pretty much see anything we want to. And beta, we were all out there today, you know, celebrating just like mortals. Zeus brought everyone to Rome and we're all living together and having the mostest fun! So when Proserpine spotted you and Alcie in the crowd and then saw you come in here, we followed because we have something to tell you."

"Oh!" Proserpine squeaked. "Best idea! Best idea!"

"Say, say!" Persephone cried.

"Why don't Alcie and Pandy and . . ."

"Iole," Pandy and Alcie said together.

"Iole! Why don't they all come over tonight for a Morpheus party and we can give each other facials and paint our toenails and . . ."

"Party, party, *party*!" Persephone began to chant as Proserpine joined in and the two began to play-slap at each other.

"Party!" crowed Alcie.

"We can't," Pandy said, snapped back into the reality of their situation.

"Why not?" asked Alcie, slapping at the air in front of her.

"Because we're slaves and Iole's a junior Vestal and we can't go out after dark—or alone."

"Oh, poo!" said Persephone.

"Double poo!" Proserpine agreed.

"Persephone, what is it that you wanted to tell me? Is it the reason why Zeus has brought everyone here?" Pandy asked, her brow suddenly furrowed. "Is it to help . . . or hurt me?"

"Ooh, such a serious face." Proserpine laughed.

"I know!" said Persephone. "Well, the official line is that we're here on a family reunion holiday. And as far as helping goes, that I *don't* know. Zeus and Jupiter are calling the shots and it's sort of a day-by-day thing. They both really want you to do this all on your own. But, yes, everyone knows about Hera, and that's why we wanted to talk to you."

"First of all, good for you!" said Proserpine.

"I *know*!"

"I KNOW!"

"Second," Persephone continued, "we know that Mercury is basically pulling double-messenger duty while Hermes is going back and forth to Persia to pick up Hera's pieces. Sandals! You turned her into sandals! Oh, Hades, don't you just love it! Zeus is telling Hermes to go slow which is why you haven't seen her yet, but she'll be restored any day now. And combined with Juno's powers, she'll be even nastier . . . we think. We wanted you to be on guard!"

Pandy stood still for a moment; they were telling her nothing really useful, only that her time was now truly running out. Hera was probably going to kill her; same old, same old, blah, blah, blah. Only now, all the gods would get to watch.

"I should get this water back to the senator," Pandy said.

"And we should get back," Proserpine said. "Speaking of guards, there was a gorgeous centurion who winked at me today while Caesar was talking. And I saw him pushing people aside with his sword to get to where we were standing before we disappeared. I wanna find him!"

"You're a married goddess!" laughed Persephone.

"So are you and I've seen you looking!"

"Okay, honey," Persephone said, turning to Alcie.

"Everyone on the underworld food-prep staff says hello. Now, protect your friend and share the goodies. We'll try to be in touch. Oh, I have *missed* you!"

"Me too, you," Alcie said.

"I know!"

"Bye, Pandy, bye, Alcie! See you," said Proserpine, as the goddesses faded into nothingness.

"Well, now you've met her—them!" Alcie said as they walked back into the amphitheater.

Suddenly it struck Pandy: the bizarre thing that Persephone had said.

"Alcie," Pandy said, stopping short. "Why did Persephone say that it had been a few years between visits? You were in the underworld with her only a moon or so ago. What did she mean by *years*?"

"Apri . . . ," Alcie started, then remembered her promise to herself that she was not going to swear using fruit anymore. "I mean, merciful Athena, I have no idea what she meant. It was probably nothing, because that's exactly what time means in the underworld: nothing. You saw Persephone, P, she's fantastic, but she's bonkers!"

"Yeah," Pandy said absently.

She was silent for several moments.

"Look," Alcie said, knowing exactly what was bothering her best friend. "Hera's tried to kill you before and she actually *did* kill me. It's nothing we can't handle."

Pandy stopped right before she entered the tunnel that would take them out of the building and looked at the immense semicircle of seats.

"How many people do you think this place holds?"

"Apollo's toenail if I know," said Alcie, popping a dove heart into her mouth.

"At least ten thousand people. And I'm here almost every day. If I were Hera, this is where I'd do it. Get a big crowd in here for some reason. A lot of people watching. And nobody would really know what's going on; just a goddess angry with a mortal. No one to save me. No one would say a word."

"You are creeping me out."

"Me too. Hey, let me try one of those dove thingies!"

CHAPTER SIX

Three Important Conversations in a Relatively Short Period of Time

Conversation . . . The First

Shortly after the middle of the night, Mercury, like his Greek counterpart, keenly sensitive to the stirrings of the other immortals, woke with a start to find Hermes kneeling out in the corridor, lacing his sandals.

"What is it?"

"Someone's rustling about," Hermes answered. "Come on, get up."

"Wait, wait, *wait*. Didn't you just get *back* from Persia only a few moments ago? Didn't I just hear you go into your room? Didn't you just *unlace* those things?"

"You are correct, sir; no more trips to Persia for me. But someone is moving about below. Let's go see who needs what."

"Ach! Why can't all of them just *sleep*. One night!"

Mercury sighed. "One whole night without somebody wanting something, sneaking about, sheesh!"

Tiptoeing down the stairs, they saw a light burning dimly in the food-preparation area. Cautiously, they peered around the doorway.

"You might as well come in, you two," Zeus said, his mouth full.

"We don't have enough to share," Jupiter said, his hands quickly covering the platter in front of him, piled high with the remnants of the evening meal.

"Who said anything about sharing," Zeus replied. "They're here and we have questions. It works."

"What's going on?" Hermes asked. "Do you need anything, Father?"

"Father?" Mercury asked, looking at Jupiter.

"Right now," Zeus replied, "all Jupiter and I needed was to polish off the leftover dormice, and have a little wine and a little chat. But, now that you're up, come in. You can tell us what's going on with my wife."

"Yes," Jupiter said, licking dormice off his fingers. "How far along is she? Are all the parts in place? Is the hip bone connected to the thigh bone? Is the neck bone connected to the shoulder bone? Say, you know, that's rather catchy. Hip bone connected to the—wait for it—thigh bone! Leg bone connected to the—here it comes—ankle bone!"

Jupiter got up and began to dance around the food-preparation room singing his little song until he saw Mercury and Hermes staring at him.

"Father, are you well?" asked Mercury.

"What? Supreme Rulers can't sing? Have a little fun?"

"I have only now just returned from Persia," Hermes said, looking back at Zeus, who was greatly amused by his own counterpart. "I placed the final piece, her head, with the others, Sky-Lord. Hera is all there, but not all together . . . yet."

"Where have you been keeping her?" Zeus asked.

At that moment, undetected by anyone, a dark figure slipped past the entryway and came to rest against the back of a nearby column.

"I found an abandoned insula directly over a section of the old sewers," Mercury answered. "Caesar has relocated all the inhabitants to make way for the new construction."

"It's perfect," Hermes added. "She's leaning against a couple of walls in a tiny storeroom way at the back. You have to walk a veritable maze to get there. Well, you would if you were mortal. No one has seen us coming or going."

"Excellent work, boys," said Zeus. "And no one has asked about her. No one misses her. Fascinating."

"Not entirely true," said Jupiter, sitting back down at

the table. "Juno has been sniffing around; I don't know how much longer I can put her off."

The figure behind the column leaned in, straining to catch every word.

"Do you think she suspects anything?" Zeus asked.

"If she does, she should go onstage with a chorus behind her; her acting is that good," Jupiter replied. "She's curious and a little ticked off that she's the only one who doesn't have her counterpart here. But, I think our story is a good cover: Hera is off visiting family, making a few stops at some of her temples and she'll be here in time for the big feast at the home of Lucius Valerius, or when and if Pandora manages to capture Greed, whichever comes first."

"It's a little illogical," Hermes said. "I mean . . . I only mean . . . that we don't know when or if Pandora will ever discover where Greed is hiding."

"Yes, well, the wife has bought the story thus far and that's good enough for me."

In the dark shadow cast by the column, the figure tensed slightly.

"Beauty and War, at my suggestion," said Zeus, "have cooked up a nice little plan. Just a little nudge for the girl. They're trying it out tomorrow morning. If it works, Greed should be in the box very, very soon. Possibly even before the feast. No muss, no fuss. And Pandora might be able to journey to her last destination before you reassemble Hera. And that would so disappoint my better half."

"You like this girl, don't you, Brother?" asked Jupiter.

"At first I didn't," Zeus said, a smile beginning to play across his lips. "You have no idea what I wanted to do to her—the punishments, the eternal tortures I wanted to inflict on her for releasing the great and lesser plagues upon mankind and the world. When she accepted the quest, I thought she would be dead within the week and then Hades could deal harshly with her while I figured out what to do about all the evils. But Pandora has not stopped surprising me: her cleverness, ingenuity, and, above all, her courage have actually made me rethink the nobility of mortal man. Or, maiden, as it were."

"Let's not forget her friends," Hermes said.

"Indeed," said Zeus. "Let us not. Here's to them."

Zeus raised his goblet and drained the last drops of wine.

Leaning against the column, the figure disappeared.

Conversation . . . The Second

"Hi," whispered Iole, sticking her head into Pandy and Alcie's tiny room. "Melania's asleep and I wanted to ascertain where you both disappeared to today. One instant I think I see you two on top of a fountain, and the next, you've vanished. Then I see you two sneaking toward the Theatre of Pompey. Exceptionally exciting about Homer, huh!? I'm thrilled and relieved I didn't see the actual battle . . . what is keeping both of you from paying the slightest bit of attention to me?"

"Huh?" said Pandy, turning. "Oh, hi, Iole."

"Hello. I half expected to run into you in the corridor going into Lucius's private rooms to do whatever you do in there."

"I haven't had time to straighten his things from the day today. Hang on," Pandy said, fidgeting with something in her hand.

"She's trying for the, like, billionth time to talk to her dad, even though it's so late back home, everyone will probably be asleep," Alcie said, curling her knees up underneath her as she sat on her sleeping cot.

"Oh! I'll be quiet."

"I don't care if it's late," Pandy said. "He might still be up."

Pandy, as she had done every few moments since she and Alcie had retired to their room that night, ran her finger down the lip of her special, enchanted shell. Then she held it to her ear and waited. As before, nothing. She was just about to run her finger over the lip again, thereby ending the call when she heard a rustling, like the crinkling of parchment, on the other end.

"Hello!" she cried, then muffled her voice. "Dad! Dad! It's me!"

"Uh, hello?" said a young, unfamiliar voice on the other end.

"Dad?"

"Uh . . . who's this?"

"Who is *this*?" Pandy asked, now afraid that her father had somehow let his shell fall into strange hands.

"This is Xander," said the youth.

"Xander who?" said Pandy, her mind not focusing clearly.

"Xander, only son, only child of the Great House of Prometheus," the boy said very fast and with a sigh, as if bored by saying it whenever he introduced himself.

"What? Who *is* this?" Pandy exclaimed.

Suddenly, there was a sound of exasperation on the other end and then Pandy heard nothing.

Immediately, she ran her finger again over the lip of the shell.

"Something's wrong," she said to Alcie and Iole. "Really wrong."

"Yeah?" said the youth when the line opened on the other end.

"Listen, don't touch the shell again, please. I am trying to speak to Prometheus, my father, and . . ."

"Okay, well, I don't know who you are, but my dad only has one child and that's me and he can't talk to you anyway."

"What do you mean, 'one child'?" she asked, getting perturbed.

"I had a sister but she died and, like, I don't even know you."

And that's when Pandy lost her grasp on every word she ever knew. She peered into the corner of the small room, seeing nothing, unable to comprehend. Alcie and Iole saw her mouth moving wordlessly; her fingers clenching and unclenching around the shell. Alcie got up off her cot and circled in front of Pandy for a better look. Iole followed and together they stared down at their best friend whose eyes were as large as bowls of cream.

"Where's my dad?" Pandy asked softly after a long pause.

"Where are *you*?" the youth asked sharply. "And how are you doing this?"

"Xander . . . this is . . . it's . . ." Pandy faltered. "Just answer one question, okay?"

"What?"

Persephone's face floated in Pandy's mind; her odd use of the words "years."

"How old are you?"

"Who *is* this? Why do you want to know?"

And suddenly, without warning, Pandy found her

resolve and her focus. She shook off the fuzziness all around her and stared into Iole's face. Then she looked right into Alcie's eyes as her brain pushed an answer up her throat and out of her mouth. She needed this boy to confirm the information she already knew was the truth. So she lied.

"This is Athena, boy," Pandy said with authority, her voice deep. "Certainly you know who I am."

"Uhhhh. Hi," said Xander, the cockiness now gone.

"I have enchanted the shell you hold so you may hear my voice. Now, answer my question: how old are you?"

"Thirteen."

Pandy's breath caught in her chest.

"Where is your father?"

"He's sick."

Pandy paused.

"How sick?"

Alcie grabbed Iole's arm.

"He can't move or talk anymore. He sleeps a lot. He can't die or anything."

Pandy fought to keep her voice even and low.

"How long has be been sick?"

"I dunno. Maybe, like, ten years. Maybe. They say he got sick when my sister died."

"And now he can't talk?" Pandy asked.

"Nope."

"How did your sister die?"

"I dunno. She wasn't here."

"How did you find the shell?" asked Pandy, her mind trying to move to something she could envision.

"I just found it behind a cushion on the floor. I heard it making noise. I guess it's been here for a while."

"And you're at home—I mean, in your home—now?"

"Yeah."

"The shell belongs to your father, Xander. I want you to take it over to him and put it next to his ear. Okay?"

"Okay."

For the next several moments, as she listened to her little brother get up off the floor cushion, walk up the stairs of her home back in Athens and into her parents' sleeping room, Pandy hung her head and took in deep breaths, trying not to panic. Alcie put her hand on Pandy's arm and Pandy grabbed it tightly.

"Dad," she heard Xander say from a distance. "Dad, Athena wants to talk to you. Okay, I'm putting it up to his ear now."

Pandy listened for a moment, trying to catch any sound. At first she heard nothing. Then, ever so faintly, she heard a delicate rasping breath—like a single leaf blown down a street by a gentle wind.

"Dad . . . ," she said, fighting like Hercules to keep her voice calm. "Daddy, I'm here. I'm alive, Daddy. I don't know what's happened, but I'm *not* dead."

She heard the sound of someone trying—and failing—to sound out words on the other end.

"Daddy! Listen to me, I'm alive. It's Pandora and I'm *alive*! I'm coming home, Daddy. I'm coming home as soon as I can!"

"Hey!" she heard Xander yelling in the background. "Hey, what are you saying to him! Dad? *Dad*, you okay?"

She looked at Alcie and Iole, now both truly frightened, and collapsed into a sobbing heap on the sleeping cot. Alcie took the shell away from her and held it to her own ear: silence. Then she ran her finger down the lip and sat next to Pandy on the cot.

"P?" Alcie said. "What just happened?"

"Xan . . . Xan . . . ," she choked out. "Somebody who said he was Xander said that he's *thirteen years old* and that my dad is sick. Really sick! He wouldn't talk to me . . ."

"Yes, well," said a deep, familiar voice from the opposite side of the room. "I think some of the blame for this lies with me. Not all, mind you, but some."

Conversation . . . The Third

Pandy, Alcie, and Iole turned to see Hermes, crouched into a ball so that his huge form wouldn't knock out the walls and ceiling of the little room. There was no blinding flash to alert them of his presence and, at this point, no one felt like kneeling or paying any kind of homage to the god. Alcie and Iole simply stared, too worried about their friend. But Pandy looked at him with agony and the tiniest hint of reproach.

"*You?*" she asked. "You knew my father was sick?"

"No," he said, shifting and trying to find a more comfortable position. "Not that. I didn't know that. Listen, you know—and you're lucky—that most of the evils in the box landed somewhere in your time—and in the *same* time. But there were a couple that kinda bounced around. Look, I don't have to tell you that you didn't just release a few little bits of nastiness. These are some of the most powerful forces known to man and gods alike, all right? And because they're the 'Big Bads' they don't necessarily follow the rules of time. They're timeless. Remember how you had to go back in time when you were looking for Lust? Roughly thirteen hundred years or so? Well, this evil, Greed, went forward in time. Not much. Only ten years. But when I brought you here, I had to take you all ten years into the future."

The girls just gaped at Hermes.

"We didn't think . . . I mean we didn't think it would be such a problem, you know what I'm saying?"

"And you didn't *think* it might be sorta—smart—to tell me?"

At any other time, Hermes might have told Pandy to watch her tone, possibly by turning her into a rabbit or a lizard for a few moments just to get his rather powerful point across, but he saw the desperation on her face and restrained himself.

"No, Pandora, we didn't. Well, Zeus didn't think it would matter and I didn't press the subject. I guess we all forgot about your conversations with your father and that this might make them somewhat awkward."

"Awkward!" Pandy chuffed, with a bitter laugh. "Great Hermes, my father thinks I'm *dead*! Ten years have gone by without any word from me and now he's . . . he's . . ."

"I'm sorry," Hermes said. "Truly, Pandora. But if you manage to capture Greed, I feel certain—kinda—that this mess might possibly be cleared up. And I can tell you that the day counter on your map still reads the same; ten years have not altered that. So . . . good times, eh? No pun intended."

No one laughed.

"Well then . . . I'm off," he said. "I have been rather busy lately, but if I get a moment, I'll try to check on your father. No promises, okay? But I'll try."

Without waiting for a thank-you, which Pandy had no intention of saying, Hermes disappeared.

Pandy turned and looked up at Alcie and Iole; her eyes were wet and her lower lip was quivering, but her voice was steady.

"My father is really, *really* sick and my baby brother is a . . . a . . . youth. I just found out that I have lost out on ten years of everybody's lives that I don't want to miss. Saving the world is one thing, but we gotta get home!"

CHAPTER SEVEN

Overheard

"I shouldn't go in," Alcie said, pausing outside the entry-way to the private chambers of Lucius Valerius. "You go and put Grumpius Maximus's water pitcher on his table, get all his scrolls and stuff ready for tomorrow, figure out which oversize pin he's going to use to keep his cloak from dragging on the ground. Y'know, page-type stuff. And I'll just wait out here."

"Don't be silly," Pandy countered. But Alcie could tell her best friend's thoughts were far away from the home of Lucius Valerius; Pandy was still very much in shock. "Everyone is asleep, so no one will know. Besides, there's so much junk in there, I need you to hold a second candle for a little more light. I have a full pitcher here. C'mon, Alce, just do it."

"Why do you have to keep it full?"

"Because he likes a drink of water first thing in the

morning. He doesn't want to have to wait while I fill it up. Simple."

"Sounds like a camel."

"Well, he sure drinks like one, and it's more and more every day. I bring him water so much, I don't do anything else when I'm with him."

"Weird," Alcie said. "Sounds like he's sick. You don't suppose . . . nah, it's too crazy. Okay, so go in and tidy up. I'll be here."

"Look, Alce, it's so crowded in there with swords and statues that I've even tripped over stuff in the daylight. And after talking to Hermes, I can't really think straight. Come on, it's not like you're a thief or anything; you work here too."

"Well, when you put it like that," Alcie said. "Plus, I can always blame you if we're caught. Say you made me do it. Heh heh."

"Yeah, say that," said Pandy absently, moving into the room.

With Lucius's water pitcher in one hand and a taper in the other, Pandy began to weave her way through the maze of objects that littered the floor. Alcie was right behind her, holding a second candle high and trying to be silent, when she smashed her big toe into the base of a small marble pedestal, nearly toppling a bronze bust. She bent over in agony and was about to scream, but Pandy instantly set down her light and put her own hand over Alcie's mouth. Alcie clutched her toe, bobbed up and down for a moment, and then was still.

"You okay?" Pandy asked.

Alcie nodded her head.

"I can let go?"

She nodded again.

Pandy took her hand away and Alcie hissed out an exhale through gritted teeth.

"My toe is going to fall off!" she whispered.

"No, it won't, but it's not going to be pretty for a few days," Pandy said, reaching the writing table of Valerius and setting the pitcher down. "Okay, done. I'll get up early and set out everything else. Let's get some sleep."

At that moment, Pandy caught the flash of another light in the corridor and the sound of a heavy footstep.

"Gods!" Alcie said, hearing it as well. "Whoever it is is coming in here!"

"C'mere!" Pandy said, dragging Alcie to a small alcove cut into the wall just behind the table and pulling the curtain fast across the opening.

"Don't make a sound," Pandy mouthed. Then, she quickly blew out their candles, plunging them into darkness. As whoever was in the corridor entered the room, the smoke from Alcie's candle drifted up into her nose and she felt herself begin to sneeze. Pandy put her finger under Alcie's nose until Alcie nodded her head, then Pandy took her finger away.

And Alcie sneezed.

Only she sneezed inside her head; she didn't make a sound. But she saw stars; her mouth fell open and her eyes crossed. In the middle of what might very well be mortal danger and with the tremendous shock of her father's condition still resonating in her system, Pandy had to bite her tongue to keep from laughing.

Whoever was in the room had now arrived at the table and was sitting easily, as if he or she knew the configuration of the room well. Then there was the sound of water being poured into a cup and the sound of someone gulping and swallowing. There was no further movement for a long time, only a sigh now and then and a bit of finger drumming on the tabletop.

Whoever it was, was thirsty . . . and impatient.

Suddenly, from around the sides and under the privacy curtain, there was a brilliant flash of light.

"Gracious One," they heard Lucius say from his seat. His voice was deeper than usual and sounded very tired. Pandy gripped Alcie's arm.

"Status report?" said a voice that nearly caused Pandy's knees to buckle. She dug her fingers into Alcie's arm until Alcie had to pry them out. Pandy leaned and whispered into Alcie's ear.

"*Hera!*"

Both Pandy and Alcie voluntarily slowed their breathing and locked their legs.

"What do you know?" asked the goddess.

"Caesar revealed the aureus today," Lucius began. "He held it up to the gawking eyes of the grotesque populace without the permission of the Senate!"

"He doesn't need you or your silly Senate," replied the goddess with a laugh, at which point Alcie gently poked Pandy in the ribs.

"*Not* Hera," she whispered.

"All the gods admire that about your new ruler, Lucius. He has the arrogance of an immortal, but it's well deserved. Me, I like dealing with mortals who're a little more wishy-washy and bendable. Weak . . . like you. If I had felt for an instant that Caesar would have agreed to my bargain I would be dealing with him now, not you. As it turns out, Caesar didn't need my help to attain the highest office in the land. Unfortunate for me."

"If Juno will allow me to continue?"

"I suppose I must. Have you come up with some sort of plan now or shall I think of that for you as well?"

Lucius cleared his throat; Pandy couldn't tell what emotion lay behind the noise: frustration or fear.

"Caesar also announced that from now on, the aureus will bear the likeness of the ruler of Rome. It's not simply his bluster in the Senate anymore; he has decreed it to the entire citizenry; it's law! And so I have already arranged for the engraver—an artist by the name of Varius—to be taken from Caesar's home and placed in . . . let's just say, a secure location, where he will either create a new aureus with my likeness on it or he will be put to death slowly and painfully."

"A kidnapping?" asked Juno. "All that commotion? Will it not wake the rest of the household, perhaps even Caesar himself?"

"The artist is housed in a small building at the back of the insula. It is used for storage and houses the slave lavatoriums. No one will hear; and beside this, Caesar and most of his entourage were and still are feasting at another senator's house this past evening. No one is at the insula except the artist, two or three house slaves—old women, and the ruler's new stableboy who also happens to be my gladiator whom Caesar stole from me today. I may have to kidnap him as well."

"No, no . . . patience, Valerius," he thought to himself. "Just a few more days."

Alcie flinched and grabbed Pandy's hand.

"I like it. And Hera will like it, once she hears of it," Juno said after a moment. "But don't play coy with me, mortal. What do you mean by 'secure location'? You will have no secrets from me."

"We are taking Varius from Caesar's insula in Subura . . ."

"You know, that's the one thing that bothers me about your ruler," Juno interrupted. "He's not yet built a royal palace on the Palatine Hill, preferring instead to reside in the same garbage dump he was raised in. I don't care if it is the largest, tallest insula in Subura. It's silly. Common. Go on."

"That's why he should never have *become* ruler. He's stupid and showy in his commonness," Lucius spat.

"My, my," Juno smirked. "I haven't seen such a hunger for power—or anything, for that matter—in ages. Normally I like it, but on you it just looks foolish. Ah, well, since beggars—even immortal beggars—cannot be choosers, continue before I grow bored: you're taking the artist . . ."

"Yes, from Subura to . . . well, as I said, his quarters also house the slave lavatoriums, so it will be relatively easy for my men to remove a few stones, create a nice-sized hole underneath and pull the poor young man down into the sewers. They replace the stones and no one is the wiser. The sewers are about to undergo extensive renovation so Caesar has blocked the main entrances. No one will think to look there. Of course, after the feast in my home when I unveil the new coin, no one will think to look at all. With my likeness on the aureus, the Senate and the citizenry will have no choice but to hand me the imperial crown. It must be done by Caesar's own decree! Caesar will be executed and I—"

Lucius's voice broke.

"I will be ruler of Rome!"

"And then the fun begins. Let's go over the bargain again, shall we?" Juno said. It sounded to Pandy and Alcie as if the goddess was now pacing about the room.

"Once I am supreme ruler . . . ," Lucius began.

"*Excuse* me?" Juno squeaked, her footsteps halted.

"Of Rome! Only of Rome."

"That's better."

"When I am ruler," Lucius said, as if he were biting down on a sweet apricot cake, savoring each word, "I shall double the number of armed guards. Then I shall order the destruction of all temples and the death of all priests and priestesses of every deity except yours. The new guards will see to it that my orders are followed and anyone who tries to intervene will be executed as an enemy of the state. Then I shall triple the number of temples to you, my queen. I shall decree that any and all sacrificial fires burn only for you, that only your statues grace homes and gathering places. Your star will shine brighter than any other in the heavens. Even moreso than that of your husband!"

"And with respect for his power greatly diminished," Juno said, "it will be a simple matter to take his power for myself. Once I am secure as the most powerful immortal, we shall help Hera to take the place of Zeus in the hearts and minds of those ridiculous Greeks. Then, finally, the world will begin to run right!"

"If I may be so bold as to inquire?" Lucius said.

"Yes?"

"Where *is* Hera? I know she is instrumental to our . . . your plans. But you have told me the Greek gods have been in Rome for some time; why does she not help you now?"

"Because," Juno voice quieted, but her words became clipped, "I have only tonight discovered that my lovely counterpart lies in pieces in a storage room underneath some abandoned insula. I have been played for a fool, lied to for days as to her whereabouts; told that she was off visiting temples and the like. And yet all the while I have felt certain that something was terribly amiss. Hera and I have been in almost constant communication for the last several weeks about her plans for the destruction of that brat, Pandora, including her intention to follow Pandora to Persia. But I have not heard a peep in days, and then the Greek contingent began to arrive and along with them, the lies."

Pandy looked at Alcie, both realizing the amount of hatred aimed at them was now doubled.

Juno sighed.

"No matter in the long run, I suppose. Everyone who has stood against us will suffer. Very well, your plans are in motion. And so are mine. In a very short time, you will rule this city and I shall rule the earth and sky. Stay true to your course, Valerius. Don't make me have to turn you into a tree frog and find someone else."

"I will not fail you, Gracious One."

"Good, although I'd like to see you hopping about in a tree. I think Caesar himself said something about it earlier today. Amusing image. We shall speak again soon. Farewell."

There was a flash of light under and around the sides of the curtain and then . . . silence. Pandy and Alcie heard more water being poured and the sounds of drinking. Then Lucius began to mutter as he made his way out of the room.

"I wonder if she's as revolting in Greece . . ."

CHAPTER EIGHT

Into the Night

"You know, you both didn't have to come with me," Pandy said softly, as two centurion night guards walked by slowly on patrol.

"Exactly what do you mean by 'both'?" asked Alcie, craning her neck to peer out from their hiding place beside a large doorway. "Do you mean that neither of us had to come with you or that you would have preferred only one of us to . . . to . . ."

"Accompany," said Iole from behind Alcie.

"Thank you," Alcie huffed. ". . . accompany you, Pandora, and if so, which one?"

"Stop it, you goof," Pandy said.

"I wasn't going to be kept from seeing my Homie."

"And I wasn't going to miss seeing Alcie see Homie," Iole said.

"I know," Pandy replied. "I've just been so . . . so . . .

Iole, what's the word for not feeling like doing anything?"

"Unmotivated."

"Right, unmotivated for days, that the first time I do feel like taking action, it puts you two right back in danger."

"Danger is my second-to-last middle name! Bring it on!" Alcie said, following Pandy as she stepped out into the now empty street and slashed at the air in front of her in a mock fight.

"Shhhhhh!" Pandy cautioned.

"Iole, are you sure we're still going the right way?"

"I told you," Iole said. "Melania was very specific about where Caesar grew up. Subura is just ahead. There are a few older Vestals we come to visit, we bring ginger cakes, et cetera. I know the route."

"I know what you told me," Alcie said. "It's just hard to imagine that Caesar likes living in this pit."

"Guys, quiet," Pandy said, scanning the buildings. "Okay, we're looking for the biggest building we can find."

"I wish there were more of a moon tonight," said Iole.

"They all look the same to me," Alcie whispered.

"There!" said Pandy, her finger pointing.

Across a square, a black form rose up behind a large

building, nearly invisible against the night sky. Pandy led the way around several corners until the insula was only a few meters away. But all was dark and silent inside. Pandy was desperately trying to determine a way in when they all heard the sound of scuffle, then a horse's whinny farther down along the road. Creeping quietly along the front of the insula, they came to a narrow alley where they all saw a light spilling from a small doorway into a wooden stable.

"Come on, horse," a voice said, low but clear. "I have to sleep here, too. Don't take up the whole stall. We have to share!"

"Homie!" Alcie nearly shrieked, and ran down the alley.

She moved so fast that when Pandy and Iole finally reached the doorway, Alcie was already holding a very surprised Homer tight in her arms—although they didn't go quite all the way around his waist.

"You have no idea what I have been going through, Homie," Alcie said. "Pandy and Iole were worried too. But I . . . I thought I'd . . . And then, today, when we saw you fight, I thought that if you lost I was just going to take the end of my palm fan and plunge it right into the senator's heart for sending you away. And then I'd do the same thing to that walking sack of ooze, Rufina! But then, you won! Okay, you didn't win, but you're alive!

Oh, Homie, I was so proud of you, wasn't I, Pandy? Wasn't I proud?"

"Very proud," said Pandy.

"Hi, guys," said Homer.

Pandy stood still for a minute, then rushed in and threw her arms around Homer and Alcie as far as they would go. Iole joined in, realizing that, since she'd become a Vestal, she hadn't really had any physical contact with anyone; she hugged everyone as hard as she could.

"How'd you guys find me?" Homer asked.

"We saw Caesar mouth the word 'stable' when he took you away from Valerius," Alcie said. "And since this is Caesar's home . . . had to be, right?"

"Alcie and I also overheard Valerius talking to Juno tonight about a plot to kidnap the artist, Varius, that Caesar's had living and working here. It's a long story, but I think it has something to do with Greed."

"You mean the guy who's living out back?" asked Homer. "The guy who carved Caesar's face on the new coin? I ran into him when I was watering the horses earlier; seems like an okay youth."

"Lucius Valerius is going to kidnap him and force him to create a new coin with Lucius's face on it," Pandy said, speaking rapidly. "Lucius is somehow gonna make a switch and Caesar will present the new coin at the final feast, which will then force the Senate to make Lucius ruler; and it only gets worse from there. Oh, by the way, we're ten years in the future, but right now, we have to stop the kidnapping. Where's the little building?"

"I'll show you," Homer said, grabbing a lamp and leading the way back out into the darkness.

"We're *what* in the future?" he said, stopping halfway across a barren patch of dirt.

"That took too long even for you, Homie," Alcie said.

"Later," Pandy said acidly, moving ahead of him. "I'll explain it all later; or maybe I'll just get Great 'We Didn't Think It Was Important' Hermes to tell you."

The first door of the little storage shed was open to the touch; Homer swung it easily back on its crude hinge revealing only blackness beyond.

"Not a good sign," Pandy said.

"He might be asleep," Alcie offered.

Once inside, Homer's lamp gave a dim light, but it was all they needed to see that the artist's room was in utter shambles. His sleeping cot was overturned as were the table and two chairs. His engraving tools were strewn all over the floor, a privacy curtain from his room to the next was lying in a heap off to one side as if it had been grabbed at, and a plate of food had obviously been flung against one wall, remnants still clinging to the mortar and stones.

"Look!" said Iole, pointing to the floor.

Two long lines were dug into the dirt with a messy collection of sandal prints on either side. They followed the lines from artist's room, through three storage rooms, and finally into the lavatorium where Pandy took the lamp from Homer and began to check the stones close to the floor.

"Here," Pandy said, motioning for everyone to look at six large stones, which, judging from the loose mortar around them, had been hastily replaced.

"Gods," Homer said. "They took him down *there*? How come I didn't hear anything? I would have helped him!"

"They dragged him," said Pandy. "From room to room. All the way."

"That means he was unconscious," Alcie said.

"You couldn't have done anything, Homer," Iole said, touching his arm gently.

"Not a chance," Pandy agreed. "These men—the ones who work for Lucius Valerius—Homer, they're good at this. I have heard about men like this when I've heard Lucius talk about Rome's past. These are the same kind of men that were used during proscription; men who would sneak into a home at night and the next morning, someone was just *gone*. The neighbors didn't hear, sometimes the family didn't even hear. These men were that good. Just like the ones tonight.

And they would have killed you, Homer, without a second thought."

"I'm glad you didn't hear them," said Alcie.

"What now?" asked Homer, visibly disturbed at not having come to Varius's aid. "Do we follow them?"

Everyone looked at Pandy, who was silent for a moment.

"I'm going," she said at last. "Alcie, you and Iole get back to the house."

"As if!"

"I am dumbfounded into near silence that you would actually think we would let you proceed without us," Iole said dryly.

"What she said," Homer agreed.

"Well . . . then we can't," Pandy sighed. "We can't tonight, anyway. We left the senator's house well after the middle of the night. If we follow now, it could be hours before we find the right path down there and we have to be home before the sun comes up. Alcie, you remember that slave girl? The one they caught outside the house after sunrise? Rufina accused her of trying to escape and you remember what they did to her?"

"I woke up shaking just the other night thinking about it," said Alcie softly. "I have never heard anyone make sounds like that."

"It's rumored that she still can't walk," Iole murmured.

"Okay, enough," Pandy said. "If it were just me, I'd go, but I won't do that to you two. We'll try again tomorrow night. The artist will need more than just one night to create a whole new coin and they wouldn't kill him before then. Would they?"

"It's doubtful," Iole said. "But we should waste no time tomorrow evening."

"And I'll see if I can't learn anything from the senator during the day," Pandy agreed.

They headed back toward the stables and the alley that would lead them to the street. All at once, they saw a light moving in the stables and heard a horse whinny from inside one of the stalls. Homer rushed into the stall ahead of Pandy, Alcie, and Iole. Just as Alcie was about to turn the corner into the stall, a voice rang out: clear and oh-so-girly with just a touch of malice.

"Hi, Homer!"

CHAPTER NINE

Rufina

Pandy yanked Alcie back from the stall entrance in the nick of time.

"Oh, I am soooo glad I finally found you!" Rufina said, sounding to Alcie as if she'd swallowed a beehive. "You have no idea how hard it's been, roaming these streets all alone. There were several guards on street patrol who wanted to take me away to someplace dark and cold, I'll just bet! Oh, let's get out of this stall with this smelly old horse. Bring that lamp!"

Rufina marched out of the stall and headed back down toward the stable entrance. She was too fast for Homer to stop and he knew she'd spot Pandy, Alcie, and Iole in the corridor. But when he went to follow her, he found the corridor empty. Passing one of the stalls on the other side, he felt some hay straws hit his leg. Looking into the darkened stall, he saw six eyes glinting back in the lamplight.

Rufina clomped into an empty stall almost directly across from the one hiding Pandy and the others; they could see everything quite clearly.

"Oh, this is much better . . . for a horse stall, that is. Where was I? Oh yes, the guards. Of course, when I told them who Daddy is, they said I was out too late for a young woman of my standing and they almost insisted on taking me home! Then I never would have gotten to see you."

They all saw Rufina move in, run her fingers up Homer's massive chest, trying to get very, *very* close. Homer had no idea what to say and was far more concerned that Alcie was going to come crashing in at any moment.

"Uh . . ."

" 'Uh, uh' . . . is that all you can think of to say to me? Hmmm? When I have walked these oh-so-dangerous streets all alone just for you? I think you should be a little glad, Homer, maybe even a little grateful. And you will be when I tell you of the plans I have for you. Oh, I have missed you so much, and I know you've missed me. I think about you all time. Do you think about me?"

"Uh . . ."

"Of course you do. I think you should kiss me now."

Alcie gagged in fury. Pandy put a hand over her mouth, but not before a tiny sound escaped. Homer stared straight ahead, pretending not to notice, but Rufina whipped her head toward the stall entrance, staring across the corridor.

"What was that? Is there someone else here?"

"Mice," Homer said, matter-of-factly.

"Mice! I *hate* mice!"

"They're all over the place," Homer replied. "Rats too."

"Great Jupiter! Hold me, Homer! Protect me!"

"I could protect you from the mice and rats," Homer said, thinking faster than he ever had before. "It's just the snakes I'm worried about."

"Snakes!"

It was then Homer realized his mistake; Rufina not only did not flee from the stables as he'd hoped, but she climbed on top of him, using his broad back as a staircase until she was sitting on his shoulders.

"Okay, good," she said. "Now anything will have to go through you to get to me. Now, where was I . . . oh, yes! Here's my plan . . ."

Homer turned Rufina away from the stall entrance and waved furiously behind his back, hoping that Pandy or anyone would see him motion them to run away.

"I know it's not common or normal—or even smart—for a young woman of my noble birth to marry a slave, but I've seen the way you look at me and you know how I feel about you and I'm sure I can convince Daddy, because Daddy always gives me what I want and I want you! He'll give us a big piece of land and a big house and once we get rid of that ridiculous Pandora and her disgusting friends, you can have her job and be my daddy's page!"

Homer began to get angry. Then he spotted something on the wall: a large hook for tying the horses' reins, or anything else anyone wanted to tie up. Slowly he began to maneuver over to the wall.

"Get rid of them?" Homer asked softly. "How do you plan to do that?"

"Oh, who cares!" Rufina said. "I'll just have them executed for any old reason. Of course Mother likes them, so I'll have to get around her but she's such a simp . . . Hey, where are you going? Are you taking me for a ride? You're sort of like my own personal horsey! Are you my horsey?"

"That's me," Homer said, turning around so that Rufina's cloak was only millimeters from the hook.

"Oh, think of the fun we'll have. We can play games like this all the time . . . *Homie*."

That was when Alcie had heard enough. She flew across the corridor and burst into the stall just as Homer deposited Rufina onto the hook where she was held fast, high, and completely immobilized.

"Nobody calls my Homie 'Homie' but me, you cow!"

"Agghhhhh!" screamed Rufina. "Get me down from here, *Homie*!"

"That's it!" spat Alcie, balling up her fist.

Pandy and Iole were on Alcie in a flash, but with strength she didn't know she had, Alcie threw them off and began rooting around in the straw.

"Oh, just *wait* till I get home! Now I really will have you executed! All of you. Even you, Vestal. And Mother won't be able to say a thing about it! Get me *down* from here, you stupid stable boy!"

Rufina reached around trying to free her cloak from the hook, with no luck.

Homer just stayed where he stood.

"You have tormented us enough," Alcie said, rising from the floor, something clenched in her hand. "You dumb, ugly, gross, lemon-rindey . . . uh . . . Iole, take it!"

Iole sighed.

"Well, since I'm going to be executed anyway, how about boorish, vulgar, impudent, ill-bred, unmannered, abusive, obnoxious . . ."

"Tough on the eyes," Homer cut in.

"Aahhhhh!" screamed Rufina.

"I have a few," Pandy piped up. "Disrespectful, rude, and something we would never be back home in Greece: obvious!"

Rufina narrowed her eyes and spoke low.

"You're all dead."

"Then this won't matter," Alcie said.

She walked forward and, reaching high, smeared a handful of horse manure all over Rufina's face.

"As they say, you are what you eat!" Alcie said, with a smile.

Rufina wanted to scream but was afraid to open her mouth.

Pandy walked to Homer and motioned for him to lower his head.

"Valerius's house, tomorrow night. We'll meet you in the garden when it's safe," she whispered into his ear.

Homer nodded.

"Give us a decent head start," Pandy said aloud to Homer. "Then call for the guards."

"They'll never believe you, stable boy!" Rufina hissed though the manure. "They'll find me and I'll tell them *you* brought me here!"

"Yeah, let's think about that," Pandy said. "Caesar's house, Caesar's stable boy. Obviously a Caesar favorite since the ruler himself freed him from the ring just today in front of thousands of witnesses. You, roaming the streets, meeting up with night guards who'll say that they saw you heading this way—alone—after a decent hour. Who will they believe? Homer will say that he had to put you up there just to keep you off him."

"After you fell in a pile of horse poop," Alcie said with a little wave.

"Oh, I wouldn't want to be you when your mother discovers your indiscretion," Iole said.

"See ya!" said Alcie.

And with a single glance from Pandy to Homer, who nodded in return, they were gone, racing back down the alley and around the corner, tearing through Subura and Rome like they were being chased by Hera *and* Juno.

A short time later, having spent every moment since their return to the house following Iole's suggestion that they press the edges of their rough cotton coverlets into their faces, Pandy and Alcie stumbled, sleepy-eyed out of their tiny room, only to crash into Melania and Iole at the top of the stairs.

"What's going on?" Alcie said, listening to loud voices below and stifling a yawn.

"Yeah," Pandy asked, stretching her arms as if she'd been asleep for hours. "What's all the noise?"

"Some sort of commotion," said Melania, starting down the stairs. "Varinia sent for us. Something to do with Rufina!"

"Rufina?" said Alcie, heading down with the others. "Commotion? But she's always good as gold!"

They found the entire household gathered in the large hall, already being festooned for Caesar's final celebration feast.

Rufina was in the middle of the floor, thrashing like a wildcat but held fast by two centurion night guards. Varinia was sobbing, held up by two house slaves until Melania crossed the floor and embraced her mistress. Lucius was circling his daughter like a tiger about to pounce on a rabbit.

"Say again!" Lucius bellowed. "*Where* did you find her?"

"The stables of Caesar, sir," answered one of the guards.

"And with whom?"

"The stable boy. A gladiator whom Caesar recently freed," replied the other centurion.

"And how do you know she was not taken forcibly from this house! I sent that youth into the ring in the first place; he could easily have wanted to revenge himself upon me by soiling my delicate child!" Lucius roared.

There were a few involuntary twitters around the room and the guards shuffled their feet and looked at each other.

"Sir, we, both of us, encountered your daughter on her way to the stables," said the first guard. "She was alone; said she was on your business, sir. A short time later, we were summoned to Caesar's home. We found the stable boy waiting for us, and your daughter . . . on a hook."

"Oh, Rufina!" wailed Varinia.

"I wasn't alone!" screamed Rufina. "Pandora, Alcestis, and the Vestal Iole were also there. Alcestis rubbed horse poop on my face!"

All eyes turned to Pandy, Alcie, and Iole.

"Sweet Minerva, daughter," cried Varinia. "I myself saw them retire hours ago."

"We haven't left our room all night, sir," said Pandy.

"Perhaps your daughter is unwell, sir," Alcie said, a look of complete innocence on her face.

"Liars!" shouted Rufina.

"Look at them, you . . . you foolish girl!" Lucius said. "Look! They still have creases from their coverlets lining their faces!"

"And you would accuse a Vestal of such behavior?" asked Melania, softly. "Perhaps she *is* ill, mistress."

"I am *not* ill!" Rufina yelled, then she dissolved into a sobbing heap. "They were there. They *were* there! Execute them . . . pleeeeeeease!"

"Take her to her room!" Lucius commanded the guards. "Wait! You, boy!"

At once, Crispus stopped staring at Iole and snapped to attention.

"Sir?"

"You will, from now on, stand outside my daughter's room. She will leave only when her mother or I allow it. You will sleep only after she has gone to bed. Is this understood?"

"Perfectly, sir."

"Retire now, all of you," Lucius went on. "Crispus, accompany my daughter upstairs. This household is to forget any of this happened come dawn."

"I am sorry you had to trouble yourselves, centurions," Varinia said, approaching them with her hands outstretched. "There's gold for each of you . . ."

"Varinia!" exclaimed Lucius, watching the gold change hands.

"I'm sure they would like to forget this episode, husband. And tongues are more likely to remain silent if they are eating and drinking well. To your health and full stomachs, both of you. May we count on your . . . discretion?"

"You may, lady," said the second guard.

"I thank you," Varinia said, watching the guards leave the house.

"Everyone, be gone!" called Lucius to the last of his household straggling up the stairs or ambling to the far corners of the house. At the top of the stairs, Pandy and

Alcie shot a look to Iole, who shot one in return before she disappeared into her closet.

"Look at the shame your daughter has brought to us, wife," Lucius said, staring at the spot where Rufina had stood.

"We paid the guards well, husband. And no one in this house will . . . What do you mean, *my* daughter? *You're* the one who has spoiled her so that she now resembles a moldy pear! You're the one who has doted upon her; you've turned her into this . . . this . . . creature!"

"Me!"

"You!"

"You dare speak to me like this!"

"Hush, you madman! Unless you want to wake everyone a second time!"

CHAPTER TEN
Profit Rolls

Just before dawn, Pandy was dreaming.

She was crawling through the belly of a snake, and yet she could stand. The stench from the creature, however, kept knocking her backward and if she tried to cover her mouth she couldn't get to her feet again because the floor was so slippery and . . .

Suddenly, Pandy and Alcie were awakened by a soft tap on the wall outside their room. An old house slave poked her head through the privacy curtain and saw Alcie on her cot and Pandy on the floor, coiled up in her coverlet.

"You are both being summoned by the young mistress."

"Well, *this* oughta be fun," Alcie said, dressing hurriedly and following Pandy out into the corridor.

They approached Rufina's room and, with a quick

nod to Crispus, let themselves in without announce-
ment. Rufina was at her looking glass and didn't
acknowledge them; she combed her hair for many
moments before deciding to speak.

"You two must think you're very clever," she said
softly. "And creasing your faces like that. Genius. Of
course, if I had been thinking clearly last night, I would
have suggested Mother or Father smell your hands,
Alcestis, but something tells me that would have been a
waste of time. Let me guess: a little rose water? Lavender, maybe? Before you went to bed?

She glanced at Alcie, who just stared back at her.

"I am going to see you both put to death—and the
Vestal too—if I have to stick you in a bear pit myself. But
until that time comes, and it will, you still have to do
what I say in this house. And I'm hungry. Only moments
ago, I heard a hawker outside the house shouting about a
new bakery. Something about the best bread in Rome,
with olives on top or some such, and I've decided to send
you both on an errand. The place is called Profit Rolls
and it's in a section of the city somewhere to the west, I
think. I don't know. Find it and bring back the household
bread for the day."

"Since Caesar is not convening the Senate today or
tomorrow, your mother is expecting us both to assist in
decorations for the upcoming feast. If we are not here
when she calls for us . . . ," Pandy began.

Rufina was on her feet so fast that Pandy didn't have time to focus. She struck Pandy hard across the face, knocking her onto the floor.

"*What?*" Rufina said, as Alcie balled up her fists and began to lunge. "*What* will you do, Al-*cesspool*-tis? You would strike me in my own home with a guard so close outside? Do you want your death to approach even faster? Stand up, slave. I've just given you a simple command and you will do as I say. Not another word."

Pandy got to her feet.

"As you wish . . . ," she began.

"*Not another word!*" Rufina screamed. "Or I will have your tongues removed and served to Caesar at the feast. Oh, and if you're not back within the time it takes me to comb the last bits of horse poop out of my hair, I'll have you declared escaped. Now, get me my bread!"

Pandy and Alcie backed out of the room, but Alcie made certain that Rufina saw her staring and that her eyes never left Rufina's smirking face.

Before heading out, Alcie asked Balbina, chief cook and head of the house slaves, for a bit of money with which to buy the bread. As she handed over the coins, Balbina cautioned both girls to be back soon; preparations were moving fast now that the feast was almost upon them and they were needed. Out of the house, Pandy and Alcie began to head west but soon realized there were many streets winding off in that direction.

"Which do we take?" Alcie asked, coming to the umpteenth fork.

Pandy was silent, looking for clues . . . anything. She even sniffed the air around her for telltale scents of baking bread. Then her eyes caught something high overhead.

An owl—beautiful, enormous, and not something she would expect to see in the bright morning sun—sitting calmly on a balcony down one street.

"There," she pointed.

At that moment, the owl was joined by a second, just as large and stunning, and they both swiveled their heads to look at the girls before taking flight slowly down the street to the west.

"Works for me," said Alcie.

"Thank you, Athena," Pandy said, hurrying her pace to follow the birds.

Within a short time, after leading the girls through a twisting maze they would never have negotiated on their own, the owls came to rest on top of a small, single-story building that looked out of place nestled between the much taller structures around it. The aroma wafting out of the open doors and windows was intoxicating and Pandy and Alcie stopped for a moment, an inexplicable feeling of both happiness and hunger creeping over them.

Walking inside, they found themselves surrounded by racks and racks of the most incredible pastries, breads, and buns. Directly before them was a long, low case with glass on the front displaying the most extravagant treats. There were cream-filled cakes, rolls with pink icing, tarts topped with peaches and honey, crispy baked "horns" filled with custard and rose petals, and tiny little dough balls rolled in lavender seeds.

"Did they have *these* in Hades?" Pandy whispered.

"Hey, don't be dissing the dove hearts," Alcie said quickly, but then she inhaled deeply and lowered her voice. "No, I don't think they did."

Suddenly, there was a tremendous clamor of metal from a back room, which could just be seen through an open doorway. Pandy and Alcie saw two men in helmets and bloody breastplates cross from one side to the other. In that same moment, Venus and Aphrodite popped up from behind the display case. At least Pandy assumed it was Venus and Aphrodite; both of the women were covered from head to toe in honey, cream, and powdered sugar. Pandy could really only tell these creatures were the goddesses by the fact that they were larger than any normal women, their golden hair cascaded in perfect ringlets, and their laughter made her feel absolutely giddy; it was the same elation she'd felt every time she'd ever heard Aphrodite speak or laugh. And now, there were two of them.

"Hades indeed!" said one goddess.

"They could only wish for delicacies such as these in Hades!" said the other. "Hello, Pandora! And . . . Alcestis, you're back! Oh, my dear girl, you have no idea how your friends mourned your, well, I guess it was a non-death, wasn't it? But believe me, Pandora wept pitchers; I still have the nose-phlegm stains on my girdle to prove it. And I *see* you're not *blind* anymore. Get it? *See . . . blind?* Oh, I laugh! Venus, darling, this is Pandora and Alcestis!"

"Greetings, you two. I've heard much, I must say."

Without warning, Aphrodite picked up a handful of powdered sugar from a bin below the counter and threw it at Venus. Then she fell back in peals of laughter. Venus responded by picking up a large tube of sweet cream and dousing Aphrodite.

"Greetings, blessed ones," Pandy said, smiling with happiness in spite of herself. "I was certain I saw you both in the procession yesterday."

"Good eye!" sang Venus.

"That was us," Aphrodite cooed.

"Uh, I have to buy the bread for the household. But since you are here, great goddesses, and we were led here, I have a feeling there's a reason. Maybe?"

Again, there was huge crash of metal from the back room and Pandy clearly saw two men beating each other with . . . something.

"Are they okay?" she asked.

"Ares and Mars?" said Venus. "Oh, they're fine. You know them, they'd argue over anything. Right now, it's over which filling to put into the fried sweet dough: crushed apples or cinnamon paste."

"Apples," said Alcie.

Pandy looked at her.

"I wasn't swearing. I vote apples."

Ares and Mars crossed the room again and Pandy saw they were beating each other with large baking trays.

"Okay, to business," said Aphrodite, flicking a spoonful of honey at Venus.

"Right, business," said Venus, ducking.

"So, yes, you're right; you are here for a reason."

"Give her the stuff!" Mars shouted, poking his head out of the back room before a large metal bowl came crashing down on it.

"We're getting to that, sweetie," Venus called back.

"Are you gonna tell her where Greed is hiding?" Alcie blurted out.

Venus and Aphrodite were silenced for a moment.

"Because that would be the only information I could

really use," Pandy said, covering for Alcie and remembering that the good will of the immortals could change in a flash. "I have to get home."

"Oh, that's right," Venus said. "Hermes told us about your conversation with your father. He came home early this morning full of remorse at not telling you about the time travel thing. Having you find out the way you did. And Zeus and Jupiter feel bad too. Well, as bad as Supreme Rulers *can* feel."

"Alcestis," Aphrodite said turning to Alcie and pausing for a dreadful beat. "Someone is still a little Miss Sassy-Toga. And no, we're not going to tell you where Greed is."

There was a sound from the back of something huge being pried from a wall, and a large clay oven sailed across the room.

"Because we don't know and even if we did we couldn't tell you," Venus said, unfazed. "Zeus and Jupiter say we're all here only to guide if necessary, not solve it for you."

"Yeah, yeah, only to help. I got it," Pandy said.

"I beg your pardon? Who's a little ungrateful?" Aphrodite asked, her hands on her large curved hips.

"No," Pandy said quickly. "No, very grateful. You have no idea how comforting it is to know you're here."

In the back room, directly in her line of sight, Pandy saw Mars whack Ares with a large sack of flour, filling the room with a white cloud.

"Glad to hear it," said Venus. "So, since we can't give you the answer, we can at least give you bread for your household."

With that, she and Aphrodite reached down behind the counter and pulled up two large sacks full to bursting with fresh baked goods.

"Right then, the long loaves are for general household consumption," said Aphrodite. "The rolls with the olives baked on top are for the spoiled daughter—*not* for anyone else. And there's a little sack with something special: sweet rolls with candied violets. Pandora, you, Alcestis, and Iole will enjoy them. There's one for each of you."

There was a long pause, during which both goddesses tried to suppress a giggle, as if each held onto a great secret.

"Oh, Dite," Venus said. "We really should tell them."

"Tell us what?" Pandy asked.

"I was going to, Nussie. I was going to," Aphrodite sighed with impatience. "Naturally, they'd never guess on their own. All right. Mars and Ares have baked special rolls for you three, which will give each of you whatever you need for six hours."

"Strength, speed, a good throwing arm, whatever," chirped Venus.

"Exactly."

"B-but," Pandy stammered, confused as she studied the little bag. "How will the rolls know what I—or we—need? Do we say it, or think it, or . . . ?"

"Oh, Pandora," Aphrodite said in a tone Alcie recognized at once. "Must we think of *everything* for you? So much has been done on your behalf. Can you not answer these questions for yourself?"

Pandy was stunned, but Alcie smiled big and bright, showing as many of her teeth as possible.

"Cool!" she called out cheerily. "Can't wait!"

"We thought these would be fun!" said Venus. "Use them wisely."

"Very well, off with you now," smiled Aphrodite.

"Uh, how much do I owe?" said Pandy, still surprised at Aphrodite's outburst and feeling somehow as if she were being rushed out of the bakery.

"Nothing. You've paid a lot in the last few ticks of the dial, so go," Aphrodite said, blowing her a kiss.

Instantly, Pandy and Alcie found themselves halfway down the street. Turning back, Profit Rolls was gone and an ordinary insula was now in its place.

"What was that about?" Pandy said, her eyes wide. "It was a simple question!"

"No, no, it's not you," said Alcie quietly. "That's what happens when the gods don't know an answer. That's the same thing Hades said to me when I was in the underworld and I asked about how I was going to contact you once I got to Baghdad. He got furious! Told me he couldn't solve *all* my problems. But Persephone knew it was just because he didn't know. And the gods don't like to admit there's anything they don't know."

"Huh," Pandy said. "I guess I never realized there might *be* something they don't know. Okay, so we'll figure out the rolls for ourselves."

"I can't remember how to get back," Alcie said, turning toward the maze of streets before them.

"Leave that to me," Pandy said, walking on. "I noticed things on the way here, like that green robe hanging on that line overhead to dry. And that missing stone in that wall over there."

Within moments, she had led them both to the door of Lucius Valerius. Alcie stopped before they went in and put her hand on Pandy's arm.

"I'll say it, spectacular. You're getting so, *so* clever; just like your dad."

Pandy sighed and hung her head.

"If you make me cry, I'm gonna slug you."

"Attagirl."

Suddenly, the front door was thrown open and Rufina

stood there, flanked by Crispus and another slave, her arms folded across her chest.

"Just about to call out the guards. You're both very lucky. Where's the bread? We're all starving to death."

Pandy began to hand her bag to Rufina, but a powerful unseen force pushed the bag back into her arms at the same time Alcie's arms were thrust forward, literally shoving her bag into Rufina's hands.

"Excellent," Rufina said, opening the bag and taking a bite out of an olive-topped roll. "Oh! Oh, yes! That hawker was right; this is the best thing I have ever tasted. Well, what are you waiting for, you stupid slaves? Take the rest to Balbina or I'll have you whipped."

Rufina turned and began to walk up the stairs as Pandy and Alcie headed toward the food-preparation room.

"Uh!" Alcie said involuntarily as she noticed Rufina's bottom moving upward.

Pandy stopped and followed Alcie's gaze.

Rufina's backside had become, in a matter of five stair steps, slightly but noticeably larger than it had been. As the girls watched, it bulged out even further, lifting the hem of her robes an extra centimeter. Pandy and Alcie blinked, trying to clear their heads.

"You see that?" whispered Pandy.

"You mean the place where she keeps her brains poofing out?"

From the food-preparation room, Balbina called for the household bread.

"Come on," Pandy said. "My curiosity will just have to wait."

CHAPTER ELEVEN
Candied Violets

That afternoon, four hundred snow white doves were delivered in ivory cages to the house of Lucius Valerius. Then came twelve thousand red and orange butterflies in a large teak crate, twenty trained monkeys, three alligators, thirty lion cubs, ten snow leopards from the slopes of the mountains in the Far East, ten black swans, and an entire family of tame white tigers. The forty elephants were tethered together in the courtyard.

"Tigers, check," Varinia said, referring to her master list. "Elephants, check. Jugglers, acrobats, mimes, and fire-eaters have all checked in. Good. Now we're just waiting for the two exotic Asian dancers with the fifteen-foot yellow python."

"Oh . . . well, naturally," sighed Balbina, surveying her once spotless marble floors.

Pandy and Alcie worked like never before, moving furniture, smashing walnuts and dates, kneading pastry dough, milking goats, polishing floors, setting out cushions, picking up swan poop, feeding elephants, beating rugs. And, all the while, glancing furtively to each other. When they had taken the second sack of bread into the food-preparation room, Balbina had found only the long loaves; no rolls with candied violets. It was several hours later that Pandy had found the bag of them, magically transported to the end of her cot, and had quickly hidden the bag below.

As Apollo and Phoebus Apollo were heading into the west, dragging the golden orb of the sun behind them, Pandy and Alcie were in the great hall sweeping the floor for the third time. All of a sudden, they heard a muffled shriek from the upper floor and a commotion on the stairs. Varinia and Balbina hurried in from the food-preparation room along with several other house slaves. Melania and Iole were the first down the stairs and into the hall, Melania's eyes searching frantically for her mistress. But before she could speak, a shape appeared behind her.

Rufina.

Who was now quite . . . enormous.

"Daughter!" Varinia cried at the sight. "Are you all right?! Was she attacked, Crispus? Is there a beehive somewhere close by? I see no stings! Rufina, why are you . . . swollen?"

"Stop it, Mother!" Rufina snorted. "You know, all you ever do is tell me to diet. 'Don't eat this, don't eat that!' Diet, diet, *diet*. Minerva's toenails, I'm awesome, and nobody *gets* it! I only had two rolls the entire day! Perhaps I'm actually undernourished, did you ever think of that, huh? Besides, I just looked myself in my glass and I don't think I've ever looked lovelier."

She glanced at Pandy and Alcie, who stood with their mouths open.

"In fact, there's a certain stable boy who might be very interested in putting his eyeballs on me right now."

"It's the rolls," Pandy whispered to Alcie. "The olive rolls. She started eating one before she even went upstairs. They had to be enchanted!"

"Yeah," Alcie whispered back. "And they're so enchanted she can't even see what they've done to her!"

Varinia cleared her throat, not at all interested in continuing the discussion with her daughter in front of the servants.

"What is it you wish, daughter? Why have you left your room? You know your father wants you to remain . . ."

"I'm going to practice my dance for the feast," Rufina said curtly, holding a sheer veil above her head.

"I don't think your father will allow . . ."

"Oh, he can lock me my in room with Cris-*pus* here guarding me until I'm dried up like a prune, but I'm gonna dance for Caesar, *Moth*-er. It's my festive and celebratory dance and I've been working on it for days. Watch. Everybody, watch!"

"There are no musicians, daughter."

"I'm going to hum."

For the next several moments, everyone in the great hall stood transfixed at the horror. Not only was Rufina achingly out of tune and a supremely bad dancer, but with her body plumped out the way it was, she was also uneven and fell more than once on her considerable backside. To keep from giggling, Pandy and Alcie pinched each other's arms until they actually drew blood.

"What's going on here?" Lucius bellowed, entering the hall. "What's that on the floor?"

"Your daughter," said Melania.

"Why is she writhing around like that?"

"She's trying to get up, dear," said Varinia. "She's practicing her dance for Caesar's feast."

"Oh. Well, fine," Valerius said, turning from the room.

"Lucius," cried Varinia. "What do you mean '*fine*'? We've scheduled jugglers, joke-tellers, and other dancers who can actually dance! You're not seriously going to let your daughter—in her condition—*display* herself like that for Caesar, are you?"

"I don't care."

"Lucius!"

"Wife," the senator snapped. "I don't *care*! It doesn't matter, do you hear? None of it matters. Pandora! Get me some water!"

Pandy dropped her broom, raced out of the room and up the stairs to the senator's private chambers, but she paused on the stairs long enough to catch his last words.

"In a week you'll be moving to the Palatine Hill, do you understand?" he shouted, not caring who heard. "You'll be happy to know that, once the golden laurel wreath sits securely on my head, I have decided to keep you as my wife even though you are far too unambitious for my liking. But that . . ."

He pointed to Rufina, struggling to stand up.

"*That* I have decided to sell to the Gauls."

Pandy and Alcie rushed through their dinner and evening chores. Each girl thought the other was making a great show of being incredibly tired; then, when Alcie fell over a chair, they realized that neither had slept much the night before. Varinia sent them up to bed early, although no one else much cared that simple slave girls had been overworked. Pandy checked and double-checked that the senator's water pitcher was full to the brim in his private chambers; if he didn't need to call for her in the morning, it might buy a little extra time just in case she wasn't actually back in the house by then.

Later, in their tiny room, they listened as everyone in the household retired for the night and the last of the footsteps on the stairs echoed through the entryway. Finally they heard the heavy front door being bolted for the night and, peeping through the privacy curtain with bleary eyes, saw the last of the downstairs lamps being extinguished.

Right on cue, they heard the soft whoosh of another curtain down the corridor being drawn aside and, within moments, Iole was padding her way toward them.

"First of all," she said softly but intently, after they were all seated on Pandy's cot, "do you know anything about what has befallen Rufina? We all saw her last night, and I'll concede she wasn't thin, but now she's the size of a chimera!"

"We think it was the rolls topped with olives that Venus and Aphrodite gave us to give to her," said Alcie.

Iole just stared at her blankly.

"Oh . . . yes. Had to be," Iole said dryly after a moment. "Venus and Aphro . . . oh, certainly."

"Let me explain," Pandy said, smiling and yawning.

"That would be appreciated," said Iole.

"We went out early this morning to buy bread," Pandy started. She related everything that happened at Profit Rolls, including the fact that there was a candied-violet roll for Iole and it would give her six hours of whatever she needed.

"And here they are," Pandy finished. "One for each. Which means, I think, that they knew you were coming with us tonight, Iole."

"There isn't one for Homer," Iole said.

"Homie doesn't need anything but me," Alcie replied, biting into her roll. "Oh, generous Aphrodite; this is insane, it's so good! All right, I need a . . . um . . . a new hair clip!"

She squeezed her eyes tight as she chewed the roll.

"Anything?" Alcie asked.

"Nope," Pandy said.

"Well, then it doesn't give you what you need," Alcie said. "But, snapping serpents, that was *fantastic*!"

"It didn't give you what you wanted," Iole said, taking a bite. "But want and need are incongruous. Pandy, anything?"

"Don't think so," said Pandy, feeling no difference whatsoever.

"I concur," Iole said. "Nothing."

"Okay, well then, we ate some flowers," Pandy said. "The house is quiet and we have to get out of here. Homer's probably down in the garden by now. Let's go."

Pandy reached into her leather carrying pouch and pulled out the magic rope. After its enchantment in Persia, Pandy had been a little concerned about the rope's powers, but it had performed beautifully the previous night, lowering her, Alcie, and Iole out of their tiny window, untying itself and then raising them all up again in the wee hours of the morning. Walking to the window, she secured the rope again. She looked back at Alcie and Iole, still sitting on her cot. Then she caught sight of her sleeping pillow and her warm blanket. She realized how incredibly tired she was and that all she really wanted to do was to crawl beneath her coverlet.

And the next instant, it was gone. All her weariness simply vanished. In its place were energy, awareness, strength, and vigor.

"Whoa!" she said, feeling the sensation melting down from the top of her head.

"Whoa is right!" said Alcie, sitting up.

"What? What?" asked Iole.

"I'm not tired anymore," said Pandy.

"Me neither . . . like, *really* not tired! I feel like I could run around the entire city!"

Pandy threw one end of the rope out the window.

"Rope, secure and hold."

Alcie let herself down first, but with such speed and agility, she was down on the ground an instant after Pandy saw her long, reddish hair disappear.

"Toss down the kid," she whispered up loudly. "I'll catch her!"

"Is she speaking about me? 'Kid'? Seriously? Can I just smack her?" Iole asked, looking out the window.

"Go on," Pandy said, laughing softly. "Rope, lower Iole."

Iole was on the ground and found both Alcie and Homer waiting for her. Suddenly, Pandy simply landed in front of them.

"I jumped," she said, tugging on the rope and stowing it back in her leather pouch. "I feel *that* good! Everybody ready?"

"I'm ready to take on the entirety of the centurion guard if they get in our way," Alcie said, running in place. "And what exactly is our 'way'? Thoughts? Notions?"

"The sewers," Pandy said, leading the way out of the darkened courtyard.

"Oran . . . ," Alcie started, then abruptly stopped herself. "I will not swear. I am a noble maiden and I will not swear. No matter if I have to wade through poo, I will not swear."

CHAPTER TWELVE

An Empty Room

"You know, I never thought I would like this," Mercury said, following Hermes along the dark, cramped corridor. "But I do!"

"Like what, Brother?" Hermes asked, expertly negotiating each corner with no light whatsoever.

"Walking!" Mercury replied. "Ambling, ambulating, trooping, tromping, traipsing, treading, stomping, sauntering, striding . . . you know, the ol' shuffle? The gentle glide? The sassy sashay?"

Hermes heard his counterpart start sliding and shuffling his steps.

"Much more interesting than simply popping in and out of someplace."

"That's why we're doing it this way," Hermes said. "I am so sick of popping I could spit. Persia, Syria, Rome. If I never pop again, I'll be satisfied. We're almost there, right?"

"Just two more corners," Mercury said. "Listen, I have been meaning to ask you something."

"Shoot."

"Well, Pandora now knows that she's ten years into the future, right?"

"Unfortunately, right." Hermes sighed.

"Which means that the rest of the world is ten years older," Mercury went on.

"Including her family, yes I know. If you're going to berate me as well, I just don't think . . ."

"No, no, you'll hear nothing like that from me, Brother," Mercury said. "The evil is in the *here and now*, not the *back then*. You did what you had to do, of course. My question concerns certain pieces of Hera. You stored her head and torso with Douban the Physician, the young boy who liked Pandora so much. Isn't he . . ."

"Older?" Hermes finished. "Yes, by ten years. Still living in the same home, still completely cooperative with keeping Hera under wraps, as it were. Under the couch was more like it. He's an even more astonishing physician than his father was. The pride of the East."

"But has he never married?" Mercury asked.

"Nope," Hermes said, stopping and turning to face his Roman self. "He and I have chatted briefly over the years, and guess what? He loves our girl. And so he's waiting. Hoping that Pandora will put everything back in the box, return to her proper time and then . . . then he plans to come a-callin', all the way to Greece. Silly humans. Silly, ridiculous passions. I told him she might be killed at any moment, but he's refused to even consider another option. Says that one look was all it took; 'Pandora or pass,' he's said for years."

"I like him," Mercury said.

"Me too," agreed Hermes, pausing. "Have you ever wished you could remain faithful like that? Loving just *one* goddess forever, or even a mortal woman—y'know, until she died? Having just that one love that makes all the difference?"

"Well, yes, certainly," Mercury said, after puffing out a breath of air. "Sure, that would be just . . . oh, who am I kidding? We're immortal. Time is no object. There are too many choices, too many bee-u-tiful creatures out there. No way!"

"Yeah, me neither. I *have* tried, but it just doesn't work for us. Still, it's a nice thought," Hermes said, turning one last corner and entering the small storage room. "Here we are."

But both gods were struck silent.

The tiny storage room was completely empty. Stunned, Hermes blew on the torch ensconced on the wall, causing it to flame brightly. But there was nothing to be revealed in the light; no pieces of Hera, no wrappings, nothing.

"Jupiter's armpits!" cried Mercury, as Hermes flung

himself from one corner to another, trying in vain to find anything. "How could she have disappeared?"

"I'll tell you how," Hermes spat, kicking at the dirt floor. "Juno! I'll bet all seven hills of Rome that she overheard us talking at some point, I don't even know when, but she found out where we were hiding her 'sister.' Now, they're both loose. The fates alone know what those two have in mind."

"Well, we have a clue . . . and it isn't rosy; not for you and me anyway. Look."

Mercury pointed high up to the corner of one wall where they saw a message written in a childish scribble with silvery blue ink:

> Errand boys, so swift, so fleet,
> Take extra care when next we meet.
> Juno's spilled all Zeus's plans,
> Like me, in pieces, in far-off lands.
> My husband, yes, will know my wrath;
> And you two boys? Stay off my path!
> First the brats will feel it most,
> Next, then, our gracious Roman host.
> And for your part in these adventures;
> Happily, we'll destroy the Messengers!

CHAPTER THIRTEEN

Circus Sewerus

Homer had to begin carrying Iole in order for them to keep up with Pandy and Alcie, so boundless was their energy. For the next hour, they all scoured the streets of Rome, looking for an entryway into the massive sewer system. Finally, when they were passing through the Roman Forum, Iole noticed a circle of stone set directly in front of a large building. It was slightly less than three meters in diameter, but there was a set of stairs leading down into the earth. Immediately, she had Homer set her on the ground.

"It might be a cellar," she mused to herself, while Pandy and Alcie jumped around in the moonlight. "But normally, in a building this large they would put a cellar entryway on the inside. It has to lead to the sewers."

Then, while Pandy tried to teach Alcie how to mimic the wheels on a chariot by throwing her feet over her hands and down again, Iole noticed many muddy foot-steps leading downward. There were also a number of tools, marble blocks, pulleys, and hoists lying behind a makeshift barricade.

"This is where they're doing all the new construction!" she thought, then she called out to Pandy and Alcie, who were playing toss with a sizable hunk of marble. "Over here . . . I'm certain this is a way down."

"Great!" said Pandy, tossing the marble chunk to Homer, who doubled over with a cough when he caught it. "Let's go get that artist!"

"Right behind you, *sistah*!" said Alcie.

In addition to tremendous energy, Pandy and Alcie, it seemed to Iole, also now had the confidence of gladiators. Gladiators who won . . . a lot.

"Hang on," Pandy said, pushing back past Iole and Homer and grabbing the first large stick of wood she could find.

"We need a light," she said, focusing her power over fire on the tip of the stick. Instantly, it burst into flame. Without so much as a glance at them, Pandy marched back into the sewer entrance and took the lead. Instantly they were plunged into a pitch black tunnel with only Pandy's torch to guide the way.

"Yeeesh!" Alcie said, hanging on to Homer's hand; actually, she was dragging him behind her since she and Pandy were moving so fast. "Okay, I'm just gonna say that I haven't smelled anything like this since I walked in on one of my cousins changing her baby's didy at a family reunion. Made me think that baby was way less cute. And that's all I'm gonna say."

"I highly doubt that," said Iole, once again being carried by Homer.

"Iole," Pandy called back, trying to walk on the upward curve of the large tunnel and not in the waste water flowing by. "You must know something about this place. If anyone does it's you, so what's up? Where do we go?"

"All right," Iole began. "The sewer system of Rome is an immense collection of huge connecting stone tunnels running directly underneath the city. Aqueducts bring water from the mountains to various public bathing houses, then *that* water is used to flush the sewers. Clay pipes take any waste away from both men's and women's public lavatoriums, some of which can seat up to one hundred people at once . . ."

"Interesting," mused Alcie.

". . . and private homes in some of the more expensive areas. Almost everything then drains into the Tiber River out of the Cloaca Maxima—or the main drain. And I have no idea which way to go."

"Well," said Pandy coming to a junction of several

tunnels. "We could be down here forever. Does anyone see anything; any light of any sort beyond the end of this torch?"

Everyone peered into the darkness.

"Nothing."

"Nope," said Homer.

"I don't see anything, per se," said Iole. "But why don't we follow the music?"

Pandy turned and held the flame up to look at Iole.

"Lovely," said Alcie. "Her roll gave her a case of the crazies."

"What music?" asked Homer.

"The music and the voices. The singing! Don't you hear it?"

"No," Pandy said.

"Crazies."

"Quiet, Alce," Pandy said. "You can hear singing?"

"As clearly as I hear you," Iole replied. "Better, in fact. And if you all cannot hear it, I would say my roll has greatly enhanced my eardrums."

"Here," Pandy said, handing Iole the burning stick. "You lead."

Iole led the way through the twisting, turning maze of the sewers. Pandy and Alcie, forced to actually stay behind Iole and not race on ahead, were wearying of plodding along in the blackness when suddenly their ears caught notes of music and an occasional shout. The next thing they were all able to discern was a dull light coming from way down one particular tunnel. As they approached the light, now spilling into the darkness from a doorway, all at once someone was thrown out and landed right in the middle of the flowing sewer.

"Now," a young woman said, poking her head out of the doorway with a grin and staring at the youth covered in muck, "you really can't come back in!"

There was a chorus of laughter behind her.

The young man was beginning to stand when he saw the flaming end of the piece of wood and then Iole's face.

"Crispus?" she said.

"Oh . . . oh, w-wow," he stammered. "Oh. Hi."

"What are you doing here? Why are you out of the house?" Iole asked, a slight panic in her voice.

"Why did those nice folks throw you into the poo?" Alcie asked.

"I could ask the very same thing about you all," Crispus replied, trying to keep his voice even. "Except of course for the poo."

"What's going on here?" Pandy said, stepping forward.

"Come," Crispus replied. "Let me show you."

He stood and wrung the water out of his clothes, then led them all to the doorway in the tunnel wall. He stuck his head in but before he could speak, a cabbage sailed out and nearly hit him in the head.

"I bring guests!" he cried.

Suddenly, the room inside became very quiet.

"Highborn or low?" someone called.

"Low," Crispus answered. "And a Vestal."

"Ooooohhhhh!" sang out a few voices.

"Let them enter," said another; the phrase was then repeated around the room.

Crispus stepped inside followed by the others. Pandy set down her flaming stick on the side of the tunnel, then actually had to shield her eyes from the brightness created by all the candles, lamps, and wall torches. She found herself in an enormous round room with a domed ceiling cut right into the bedrock underneath the city. Its circumference could have circled her entire house back home in Greece, including the courtyard and her father's small but prized olive grove. This room was jammed full of men and women, young and old, each wearing the simple garments that indicated slave status. There were a few tables and fewer chairs; most of the people were standing. In a small space in the middle of the crowd, several couples had suddenly stopped dancing; beyond them,

Pandy saw a group of musicians holding their instruments in the air, mid-note. Most of the revelers held cups of wine or other drinks; many had plates heaped with food. And all of them were now staring and whispering.

"Fellows," said Crispus, "I give you Pandy, Alcie, and Iole, the Vestal, so don't touch. These three belong, as do I, to the house of Senator Lucius Valerius."

"Then *that* must be the maiden you were just talking about!" called out one youth from back of the room, staring at Iole.

"AND *THIS* FELLOW I DON'T KNOW, SO . . . ," shouted Crispus over the youth to drown him out. "So why don't you tell us who you are?" Crispus added, glancing at Homer.

"I'll tell you," said a young girl close by. "He's the gladiator who lost but won in the ring yesterday morning. You're now held by Caesar, right?"

"Uh, right. Hi. I'm Homer."

"HOMER!" the crowd shouted.

"Welcome all," said a large man standing with an even larger woman in the middle of the dance floor. "There's food and drink; help yourselves. The evening is young and we have many hours before the cock crows. Musicians, play!"

With that, everyone returned to whatever they had

been doing—with the exception of a few looks to Iole, then Crispus, which didn't go unnoticed.

"Crispus?" Pandy said, turning to face him. "Start talking."

"What? Oh! This?" he said.

"Yeah, *this*, smelly," said Alcie. "What is all *this*?"

"Well," he started, "by day, this is a planning room for the supervisors reconstructing the sewers. But at night, it has become a gathering place for slaves from around the city. Here, we can at least have a little fun for ourselves before returning to scrubbing and milking and guarding cows."

"You don't guard any cows," said Iole.

"He means Rufina," said Pandy.

"Appl . . . ," coughed Alcie. "I mean, *hah!* Good one."

"But what about the girl?" Pandy began. "The slave girl from the senator's house who was caught outside and punished? Aren't any of you worried about that?"

"That girl had had a little too much wine," Crispus said. "We tried to stop her—even tried to take the cup out of her hand. And several people offered to walk her to the senator's house. But she wouldn't accept our help. She started back alone. Someone tried to follow her but she sensed it and eluded him. Then the next morning, the centurion guards found her sleeping in a doorway. That's how she caused herself so much trouble."

"So the masters and nobles don't know about this?" Pandy asked.

"Oh, they know all right. And they only permit it because they know it makes us happier and more productive as we toil away for them during the day if we can have a little fun on our own time. Every once in awhile, one of our masters will even join us. But the single condition is that we must all be in our masters' homes by sunrise. And we take turns just in case there is an emergency. Tonight, Tacitus and I are here while Septimus and Priscus keep watch in case the senator needs something. Tomorrow night, we will stay in the house and those two can eat, drink, and dance until dawn."

"And you never told us," Alcie said, "*because* . . . ?"

"I never talk to you," he said, glancing at Iole. "To any of you, that is. And you all have been serving the senator as long as I have. I thought you knew about this place and just decided you didn't want to be here."

"Oh," Pandy said. "You're absolutely right about that. We didn't. Well, we *did* know about it. We just thought it had . . . moved. Okay, then. We have to be off now."

"But you just got here," Crispus said as he stepped in front of Iole, guiding her a little farther away from several rough-looking slaves who were staring at her. "This way, Vestal."

"That's the one you like, eh, Crispus?" said one out of the corner of his mouth. "Not bad. Not bad at all."

"Please be quiet," Crispus begged softly to them. "Now, why do you all have to be going? You've only just arrived."

Pandy, Alcie, Iole, and Homer all looked at each other. For the first time in a long time no one could come up with anything clever or diverting.

"Uh . . . ," said Alcie.

"Yes . . . uh," Iole said, looking at Homer.

"Is there something wrong?" Crispus asked. "Something wrong at the senator's?"

Even though her enchantment still had her incredibly energized, Pandy forced herself to calm down as she scrutinized Crispus and tried to think logically; there were two possible outcomes if she were to take this youth into her confidence. He would either join them or run straight to Lucius Valerius.

"Crispus," she said, moving toward the doorway. "Will you join us out here?"

"What are you doing?" whispered Alcie.

"Maybe buying us some time," Pandy said.

Out in the large tunnel, everyone gathered around Crispus.

"How well, would you say, do you know your way around these sewers?" Pandy asked.

"Very well," Crispus replied. "When I was very young, before I was given any responsibility at the senator's, I was allowed to run in the streets with other slave children during a portion of the day. We played down here quite a lot. I know the outline of the tunnels like the back of my own hand. Why?"

"What about all the new construction?" Homer asked.

"There are some parts that are unknown, certainly," Crispus said. "But the work goes slowly. Why?"

Pandy looked at the others and took a deep breath.

"I'm gonna keep it short," she began. "It all started when I found a box underneath my parents' sleeping cot and I decided to take it to the academy for a big project . . ."

After she'd finished, retelling only the parts that were truly necessary, Crispus stared at the ground for a long time, his lips pursed together. Then he turned to Iole.

"If you don't like me, all you had to do was tell me."

"Whaaaa?" Iole started.

"I understand that I'm not much, as it were. I know I'm only a slave and you're a Vestal. Fine. But if I'd known you really despised me, I would have tried very hard not to look, not to smile, not to even think . . ."

"Crispus," Iole said.

"But to have your friend try to convince me that you're all insane is slightly beyond . . ."

"Hey, smelly!" Alcie snapped. "We're not insane! It's all true. And, just so we're all clear here, Iole *does* like you. I can tell!"

"Oh Gods," mumbled Iole as Alcie tore on.

"All we want is to get through this maze and find an artist we think has been taken down here so we can keep him from creating a whole new coin. Simple. Now if you need a little proof about everything that Pandy has told you, fine! Pay attention. Pandy, do something."

Pandy picked up the stick leaning against the tunnel wall, one end now charred black, and focused her mind. Instantly, the blackened end began to glow a faint orangey red.

"Jupiter!" Crispus cried.

"He's not here," Alcie said, feeling another energy surge and bouncing on her heels. "You lookin'?"

"Yes," Crispus said, amazed as the stick caught fire once again.

"So," Pandy said, holding the brand up to her face so that Crispus could see her eyes. "I'm not lying. None of us are. Now you know why we're here in Rome. It's a lot to . . . to . . ."

"Comprehend," said Iole.

"Thank you," said Pandy. "Comprehend, but believe me, you'll have plenty of time to think about it all later. Right now, we need your help. Can you guide us?"

Crispus looked at each of them in turn, but it was only when he looked at Iole—her beautiful little face, now devoid of any cheek blush or lip color, just her big brown eyes staring at him—pleading, that he melted.

Crispus took the torch from Pandy. "Follow me."

CHAPTER FOURTEEN
Flood

Crispus wound his way through the labyrinth of the tunnels for an hour, stopping only occasionally to caution Pandy and Alcie.

"Do you two know where you're going?"

"Nope," Alcie said.

"Then would you mind not sprinting ahead like rabbits?" Crispus said. "It only slows us down when we have to wait for you to join us again."

"Got it," Pandy said, running in place.

"So," Iole said, somehow always finding herself closer to Crispus than she might have thought appropriate— Vestal or not, "I'm ascertaining we're close to the Cloaca Maxima, correct?"

"Not really," Crispus said. "Why would you think that?"

"Because of the loud noise," Iole said, surprised.

"There's the sound of a huge rush of water and I thought it was the main drain into the Tiber."

"I hear nothing," said Crispus. "Everyone be still, please."

Pandy and Alcie stopped fake-slapping at each other and Homer didn't move a muscle.

"Nothing," Pandy said.

"Well, whatever it is," Iole asserted, "it's getting louder."

"Bellowing Bacchus!" Crispus yelled. "They're draining the baths!"

"This is bad?" Alcie said.

"Come on!" he cried, taking off like a deer.

"Sweet," said Alcie. "We get to run!"

"Iole!" Homer commanded and without a word, Iole jumped into Homer's arms as he dashed down the tunnel.

All of a sudden, there was a rush of wind at their backs along with the slight scents of sulfur, olive oil, eucalyptus, and burnt sage, and everyone heard the horrible sound. Then the wind in the tunnel began to carry tiny droplets of moisture.

"Move!" Crispus cried, although he was the one beginning to drag behind. Without breaking his stride, Homer picked up Crispus in one swift motion.

"Up . . . ahead," Crispus choked out, his rib cage

bouncing off Homer's forearm. "There's an opening—an alcove—on the left!"

Pandy and Alcie ducked inside quickly, but Homer couldn't fit through the opening without first setting Iole and Crispus down. They hurried through, but Homer made the mistake of looking back up the tunnel. The flood of bathwater slammed into him so fast, he was there one moment and gone the next.

"Homie!" Alcie screamed.

The torrent of warm, oily water was at least a meter high and rising; water was splashing against the opening and spilling into the shallow cutout in the tunnel wall, barely big enough for two people let alone five. Then, Iole clutched Pandy's arm.

"Look!" she cried.

There, clinging to the corner of the opening, were two sets of fingers, growing whiter as their grip loosened against the onslaught of water.

"Get him!" shouted Alcie. "Pull him in!"

Crispus leaned out and grabbed Homer's wrists, but his strength was no match for the current.

"I'm losing him!"

Without warning, Pandy felt an energy surge unlike any she'd felt before.

"Move, please!" Pandy said, leaning over Crispus and grabbing hold of Homer's wrists. Crispus shrank back slightly into the alcove as Alcie joined Pandy and latched on to Homer. Together, the girls hauled Homer out of the flooding river of bathwater like they were picking a piece of lint off a floor cushion. Then they settled him in the cramped space where now everyone was pressed into the rock—and each other. Shaking slightly, Homer coughed and sputtered for a bit, spitting up a small quantity of water.

"Oh, Homie," Alcie said, unheard over the din. She was trying to wriggle her arms free from where they'd become pinned behind her back. Then she realized that she'd have to poke and prod the others if she did, so she settled for just being able to rest her head on his heaving chest.

"P!?" she yelled, looking at Pandy, now scrunched back to back with Crispus. "Did you feel that? Was that amazing or what?"

"You bet I felt it," Pandy answered over the roar of the rushing water. "I felt like I could move a mountain! Gotta love those rolls!"

"I hate to interrupt you two Titans," Iole said loudly. "But we have another problem."

"What?" asked Pandy.

"Check the hems of your togas," Iole called out. "You might find them a little damp."

With all of them crammed into the small alcove, the

water splashing inside was now also rising; Iole's head would be the first to go under, but the others would soon follow.

"Crispus!" Pandy cried. "How long does it usually take to drain the baths?"

"It should have been over by now, if it was just one," he yelled. "But because the big feast is tomorrow—I mean, tonight—everyone is going to want fresh bath-water. So they're probably draining them all! This could go on for hours!"

"Oh Gods!" Pandy exclaimed.

There was absolutely nowhere to go.

Suddenly, Crispus raised his voice and began chanting.

"What are you doing? And why are you doing it *now*?" Alcie couldn't help but ask.

"Saying a prayer to Cloacina, the Goddess of the Sewers," he shot back. "The workers say it every morning when they enter the tunnels and Romans who like clean water say it all the time. Now don't interrupt! In fact, say it with me, *all* of you! 'O Cloacina, Goddess of this place, look on thy worshipers with a smiling face. Soft, yet cohesive let their offerings flow, not rashly swift nor insolently slow. Accept our offerings as all we have to give. From earth, through us, and back again! And so, through you, we live!'"

"You gotta be kidding!" yelled Alcie.

"IT'S WHAT WE SAY!" screamed Crispus.

"O Cloacina, Goddess of this place," everyone began to chant, over and over. "Look on thy worshipers with a smiling face . . ."

All at once, there was a huge jolt as if an earthquake were shaking the whole city. Iole's head went underwater for a moment and when she emerged, she was beyond terrified.

"I don't think it's working," she said through chattering teeth.

"We're making the goddess *mad* with that chant," Alcie said.

"We're not!" Crispus cried. "Keep going!"

They all raised their voices louder and the earth gave another huge jolt.

"Again!" shouted Crispus.

Then, right in the middle of the chant, the stone wall at their backs suddenly gave way as if it had been blown apart, and the five of them went tumbling backward, carried by a flood of bathwater. It went black for a moment and Pandy saw nothing, but she felt a tangle of limbs and clothing as they brushed, crashed, and swirled around her. Then, like a school of fish caught in a net then thrown onto a dock, they all skittered to a stop on a large, smooth rock floor.

Pandy spat out bathwater and crawled out from under Alcie's cloak, as everyone else also tried to free themselves from the soaking wet pile. Pandy's eyes were trying to adjust to the new light all around her and as she squinted, she saw that she, Alcie, Homer, and Crispus were splayed on the floor of an enormous cavern. Instantly, her memory recalled visions of the Chamber of Despair in Egypt and the Garden of the Jinn in ancient Persia. Like the Chamber, this place reeked with a strange smell, though not quite as overwhelming. But this cavern had three singular things that set it apart from those others.

The water, the lights . . . and the *faces*.

All around her—even on the ceiling—nearly everywhere Pandy looked, the face of a beautiful woman, the *same* woman, was carved in dozens of spots, high and low on the rough, dark gray cavern walls. There were many different sizes; some were as tall and wide as large horses, others were as small as serving platters. But out of the mouth and eyes of each was flowing a stream of water; hundreds if not thousands of liters of water were gushing per second, creating waterfalls everywhere. Large drainage pipes—from all over the city, Pandy thought—were emptying their contents here, which was of course why it smelled. Although, at this particular moment, the foul odor was being overtaken by the same smell she'd caught in the tunnel:

bathwater, bathing oil, and pungent eucalyptus; the resulting spray was not entirely unpleasant.

Trying to peer through the mist, Pandy could just make out one especially large carved face, at least five meters high, at the very back of the cavern floor. Out of the mouth flowed a wide, unending stream.

"That's the Cloaca Maxima. The main drain," Iole said from behind her. Pandy just nodded, not turning around.

The draining water dropped into deep, wide pools, which overflowed the floor of the cavern and then joined the main stream, making the cavern nearly impossible to cross. But these pools seemed magically lit from within, as if candles or lamps somehow burned brightly at the bottom of each. And each was its own brilliant color: leafy greens, blood reds, cobalt blues, lemon yellows, and on and on. The main stream, the Cloaca Maxima, was lit its entire length in the color of a pink and orange sunset as it ran at a very slight angle downward toward a great arched hole in a far wall.

"And through that hole," Iole said again, "everything flows into the Tiber."

Pandy could only imagine what the cavern would be like when the baths weren't draining, when . . . other things were being sent into the Tiber.

"The question is," Pandy said, now turning to face Iole, "how do we get out? Iole?"

But Iole wasn't there.

"Yes?" came Iole's voice out of thin air.

Pandy jumped back, nearly landing in the main drain.

"Iole . . . where are you?"

"Right here."

"Alcie! Homer!" Pandy called, motioning every one over and around the disembodied voice. "Do you see Iole?"

"Pandy, what's wrong," Iole said. "I'm standing right in front of you."

"Hate to break it to you, shortness," Alcie said slowly, coming up behind Pandy with Homer. "But if you are, you've gotten very thin."

"You can't see me?"

"Not at all," said Crispus.

"Okay," said Iole. "Okay, then this has to be the effect of the roll, correct? But why?"

"Exactly," said Pandy. "Why would you need to be invisible?"

The next instant, Pandy spotted two huge shapes moving forward through the mist. For a moment, they were unrecognizable. Then Pandy's stomach flipped over as Juno—or was it Hera?—stepped into sight.

CHAPTER FIFTEEN

Cloacina

"Hera, darling, you were right: you *were* hearing voices!"

Then Hera stepped alongside Juno, and Pandy wondered how she could ever have mistaken one for the other. Hera's brow was more deeply furrowed, her lips were just a tad thinner, and the Romans hadn't given their chief female deity as expansive a waistline. And there was a hatred in Hera's eyes when she saw Pandy that was singular and unmatchable. At least, it looked that way to Pandy.

"Oh, Juno!" said Hera, batting at the mist as she stepped on—not in—the pinkish-orange stream. "It's nowhere near my birthday, and yet you've brought me presents. Little rag dolls in the likeness of my favorite brats that I can toss against the walls, throw on the ground . . . and tear limb from limb."

"I didn't bring them here, my dear," Juno said. "I'm

guessing it was that noxious, odious killjoy we have locked up. This is her work."

"I see almost everyone I know: muscle boy, smart mouth, and the thorn in my side . . . and a stranger," Hera said, glancing at Crispus. "Poor stranger. Wrong place, wrong time."

She turned to glower at Pandy.

"Where's the smart one?"

Pandy didn't answer, not knowing exactly how to cover, but rightly guessing that Iole was, at the moment, invisible to immortals as well.

"Iole is a Vestal, sweet goddess," Crispus piped up. "She would never be caught outside at night, alone."

"Well then, let me guess!" Juno cried. "Just let me see if I can guess from your descriptions, Hera; now this one is Homer, right?"

"Right," said Hera, staring at the blond youth.

"I have no idea who this one is."

"Crispus, my lady," he said, bowing. "May I say it is an honor—"

"Shut up," said Juno. "And *this* one must be Alcestis, because you said she was prettier than the others. So that means *this* one—the plain one with the boring brown eyes—this one *has* to be . . . Pandora!"

"Right on all counts!" said Hera, clapping. "Now, once again, my little bratty-cakes, how to do it? I want to see you really suffer. So, how to do it?"

"Oh, let me help! Please!" cried Juno.

"Of course," Hera said, circling. "And why not start with the one that 'didn't take' as it were; the one Hades tossed out of the underworld. Pandora, isn't this fun? You can watch your friend Alcestis die all over again."

Pandy tried to summon her considerable strength, but found her hands instantly pinned behind her back by an enchantment.

Hera raised her arms to hurl a death blow to Alcie . . . who just stood, staring the goddess down.

"Oooh," said Juno. "See how she glares at you, Sister! The impudence!"

"Yeah, well I was blind last time, right, Queenie?" spat Alcie, although her knees had begun to shake. "Kinda easy to take down a blind girl, huh? Apri—I mean, you bet; *that* took some major courage. So *go ahead*!"

Hera's eyes narrowed into slits and her mouth pulled back into a snarl. Just then, a pitiful scream—and then another—echoed from somewhere deep within the cavern.

"The artist!" cried Juno. "Something's happened to him. Come, Sister!"

"Awwwww! But I want to kill them!"

"All in good time, darling," Juno said, hurrying back into the rainbow–tinted bathwater mist. "Let's take them all with us, shall we?"

At once, Pandy and the others felt themselves lifted

off the ground and flown swiftly through the spray. In moments, they could all see that the cavern was even larger than they thought; the entire main section had been completely obscured. As Pandy was dumped roughly on the ground, she caught sight of a chair, a work table, and Varius, pale and thin, trying to jump up and down although his feet were heavily shackled.

Juno and Hera were literally standing over him as he rubbed his backside.

"Something poked me!" he cried. "Then it *kept* poking me!"

"There's nothing here, you idiot!" Hera cried. "And *stop* trying to delay the inevitable. When you were brought here, you said you couldn't work with your kidnappers hanging around to guard you, so we changed them into eels. You said you were hungry so we gave you a crust of bread. You said you were thirsty so we gave you a sip of water. *Clean* water! You said you couldn't carve a new coin because all your tools were still in your shack, so we brought them to you. Now finish the face of Lucius Valerius or I will turn you into a Satyr that loves to drink only from the Cloaca Maxima!"

"Nice thinking," said Juno.

"I still don't know why we can't just create this coin our own sweet selves," Hera said. "Why do we need this scrawny mortal to do the work?"

"I've explained it to you already, my dear," Juno said.

"The work must look like it was humanly crafted so as not to arouse suspicion. If we did it, it would be flawless and therefore unusable."

"Right. Fine. And now, where was I?" Hera said, turning toward Pandy.

"Wait, Sister," Juno said. "I've been thinking; this whole business about not being caught outside has put an idea into my head. I think they *should* be caught as runaways! First of all, Pandora and Alcestis belong to the house of Valerius and if they're not there to help with Caesar's final feast, then a great fuss will be made about that. We must see that they're in attendance to help things run smoothly at the celebration until the time that Caesar unveils the coin of the empire. Now, we can kill Pandora and her friends anytime, but imagine the fun we'll have watching them hopping about like frightened deer, with the master and mistress of the house furious with them for being caught as runaways. And of course they'll be tortured with gruesome thoughts about how and when you and I will finally deliver their grisly ends!"

Hera just stared at Juno.

"Oh, you're good," she said. "You might even be better at this than I am."

"Flatterer. Now, let's put them someplace safe with you-know-who."

"OW!" screamed Varius. "I got poked again!"

Hera sighed and waved her hand. Varius's mouth disappeared.

"Breathe through your nose."

Juno snapped her fingers. Pandy, Alcie, Homer, and Crispus suddenly found themselves standing against one wall of the cavern, about thirty paces away from the worktable. Varius was now pleading, his hands flying, to Juno and Hera for the return of his mouth. When Pandy's head cleared from all the flying and dematerializing, she realized that it would be incredibly easy now to escape; they could all just sneak around the outer rim of the cavern until they reached the wall they'd burst through. Iole must be watching, Pandy thought; and she'd follow, of course. The mist would hide them, and if they all ran fast enough . . .

"Crispus," Pandy said, prodding the boy from his kneeling position on the floor. "Come on. We can all get out of here and get back before sunrise. Then we can warn Caesar . . ."

"Can't you see the boy is praying?" came a soft squeal from over Pandy's shoulder.

Pandy turned to see a woman standing a little further along the wall. Her face was lovely—beautiful, in fact—and very familiar. Then Pandy glanced at all the carvings in the cavern. The nose, the mouth, the almond-shaped eyes; they were the very same.

"It's . . . she's . . . you," Pandy said, pointing to the walls.

"Go to the head of your class."

But the face of the woman in front of her was dirty and her dark hair appeared to have been coiffed, but perhaps several days ago. Now some of it hung down in unkempt ringlets, and a pearl comb was tangled in a knot of hair and . . . something else. The fabric of her robes looked new, but they were beyond filthy. Then Pandy caught a downwind whiff and nearly keeled over.

"For Jupiter's sake, don't fall backward," the woman said. "You'll fry like a fish."

"What?" said Pandy, covering her nose.

The woman picked up a tiny stone and tossed it in front of her. One meter out from the wall, the rock exploded against an unseen barrier.

"Stop exploding things, Cloacina," Juno called out. "Or I'll explode you."

"I hate her," said Cloacina, her eyes narrowing as she looked at Juno. She was trying to keep her voice low, but Pandy felt somehow that this was a creature who was used to screaming. "People despise me for what I look like, what I rule over; how I smell. Yet they need me to keep their homes and their bodies clean and purified. They love me for that. No one needs Juno or that new one. The Greek sow. No one needs or loves them."

Cloacina turned back to Pandy and the others.

"You may thank me for saving you now," she said.

"I knew it!" Crispus cried, raising his head. "I knew it was you!"

"Of course," Cloacina said. "You chanted, I answered. I can't get myself out of this silly prison those two have put me in, but I can still bust out a wall and save a group of slaves from drowning in bathwater."

"Cloacina, Goddess of the Sewers," said Crispus, "this is Pandora of Athens. She's actually not a slave. She's here to find . . ."

"*I know* who she is!" Cloacina snapped, but in a way that reminded Pandy of a small barking dog. "I know who you are, my dear. Honestly, just because I live underground and my home is decorated with Rome's waste material, nobody thinks I'm in the loop, you know? Oh, sure I try to pretty it up with effective mood lighting but . . . anyway, *you're* the one all the gods are talking about. It's not that I get invited to any of their smart evening meal gatherings, mind you, but I hear things. Vibrations through the pipes and whatnot. I read a lot. I stay current. And those two blue-robed gorgons have done nothing but talk about you since they wangled their way into my home and imprisoned me. I would've liked to welcome you properly, but I'm afraid I really can't play hostess right now."

Pandy was overcome by the oddest sensation. She had become used to having her name and tales of her adventures precede her; Douban the Physician had known all about her, and Mahfouza had told her family everything before Pandy had arrived at their home. But Pandy had never been so bizarrely excited—this time, her reputation had gone before her into the sewers of Rome and into the ears of an important but isolated goddess.

"I don't mean to be rude, but why are you imprisoned?" Pandy asked.

"*They* wanted to use my underground palace for their unsavory scheme," Cloacina said, cocking her head toward the two goddesses. "I said no, so I got locked up. They caught me completely off guard—which doesn't happen often. They were all smiles one moment. 'Oh, we're just taking a tour of the sewers,' Juno said. Next moment, I'm in here. You know, I think I've seen the other one—the bigger one—before. I think she was in line at the Bureau of Visiting Deities in Persia just a little while ago. I was there on a working vacation for some genies, seeing if they could get a better sewer system in Baghdad, and that blue-robed kraken was asleep at the head of the line. What a maroon!"

Suddenly a rock exploded against the barrier—from the other side.

"Cloacina!" cried Hera. "He's almost done over here. If you cause him to make a mistake I will personally slice you into tiny bits and feed you to my prized peacocks."

"And I'll let her," yelled Juno.

"Try it, heifer!" said Cloacina. "I'll choke 'em all . . ."

"Uh! It was me!" said Pandy, as Cloacina turned to look at her. "Sorry, my bad."

"Add it to the list, brat," said Hera, turning back to Varius.

Suddenly, at the worktable, Juno gave a whoop and held up a small, shiny piece of gold. Hera and Juno both examined it in the candlelight. Then Juno set the coin back on the table as she and Hera danced about joyfully in the colored mist.

"What gives?" whispered Alcie.

"Iole," mouthed Pandy.

Ignoring the celebration over at the table, Pandy took a small step forward.

"Iole?" she asked softly.

"Here," came Iole's voice.

"Bright ideas?" Alcie asked.

"None. How about your power over fire, Pandy? Any way to use it?" Iole's voice seemed to be coming out of the mist.

"I can't think of anything," Pandy replied. "I could

turn all the water spray to steam . . . but that would only cook everyone."

Without warning, Iole materialized for an instant, then disappeared again.

"Uh-oh," Pandy said, then all at once she felt exhausted. Beyond exhausted. She nearly sank to her knees alongside Alcie, who was leaning against the rock wall. Then she found her footing again and was fine. Then Iole popped into view for a longer period of time. Then she was gone again.

"The rolls," Alcie said. "They're wearing off!"

"Which means our six hours are up and it won't be too much longer before dawn," said Pandy. "Iole?"

But Iole was already on the move. Flickering in and out of view, she was moving through the mist, trying to get close to Varius and the new coin. Then Pandy saw Iole's flickering arm from behind the large wooden chair, reaching out for the golden disk, newly engraved with Lucius's face.

"What is she doing!" Alcie gasped.

"Gods! I think she thinks the coin might be connected to Greed!" Pandy said.

"It's not," said Cloacina flatly.

"The aureus Caesar held up to the crowd wasn't, I know that," Pandy said, flickering hope that the goddess knew something more. "But how do you know that *this* gold isn't affected?"

"Please," Cloacina said with a laugh. "I deal with scary, putrid nastiness all day, every day. You think I wouldn't be able to tell when *una malorum SEMPER* came into my realm? Besides, all the things I've heard about your adventures indicate that merely touching one of the great Evils would infect the mortal touching it. And that pale kid with the tiny chisel has been hands-on with that gold for a while; he looks fine. Greed is somewhere else, believe me. And your friend is gonna get herself in trouble for nothing."

Iole's fingers were almost on the coin when she became completely solid and in plain view . . . of Hera. The goddess snatched Iole's wrist, nearly breaking it.

"Well hello, little one," she cooed. "So nice to see you. Juno, *this* is the smart one! Then again, maybe not so smart after all, eh? Oh, Pandora, change in plans! Not going to kill the redhead first. I'm going to snuff out the brains of the operation."

"Wait!" cried Juno.

"Why is someone always stopping me!" screamed Hera.

"But, my darling, she's a Vestal!" Juno said excitedly, picking up the newly carved coin and dropping it into a pocket in the folds of her robe.

"Yes, *and* . . . ?" Hera said.

"*And* do you know what they do to Vestals if found in the company of a male?" Juno said, nodding toward Crispus.

"Swat 'em hard on the behind?" Hera queried, shrugging her shoulders.

"They bury them. *Alive!*" Juno said. "And she belongs to the senator's house. Oh, Hera! If I am correct, all the other entertainment at Caesar's feast will just be an appetizer to the main course *and* a tremendous bore! We're going to see this child covered with dirt while she's still squirming!"

"Gods," yawned Pandy, in spite of her terrific panic, as she leaned against Alcie where she stood. "Juno makes Hera look like a purring kitten."

But Alcie was already asleep.

"All right, everybody front and center," cried Juno.

Instantly, Pandy, Homer, Crispus, a sleeping Alcie, and Cloacina were transported out of their invisible prison to face the blue-robed goddesses. Pandy felt sleep trying to overtake her. It had been forever since she'd closed her eyes, and all that running and jumping. As energized as she had been, that's how tired she was now. One of her two best friends was going to be put to death in the most gruesome way and it was all she could do to keep her eyes open.

"And now, two centurion guards, if you please," Juno said.

Hera held the group at bay while the Roman goddess snapped her fingers. Instantly, two guards in full armor appeared, completely confused at having been whisked off the streets above.

"You will not speak," said Juno. "You will listen."

She yanked Iole out of Hera's hand. Dragging Iole over to Crispus, she grabbed him by his cloak, holding them both out in front of her as if they were soiled garments.

"I have here a Vestal and her male companion. She belongs to the house of Lucius Valerius and you will get word to him that she has been compromised by his company and probably has been for many moons. You will take them to the prison and you will inform the captain of the guards and Valerius himself that you two found them both on the street together holding hands. Inform them as well that her sentence of death and his must be carried out after nightfall but before daybreak or the wrath of the Queen of Heaven will fall heavily upon him."

"Queens," corrected Hera.

"Very few people really know that the Greek gods are here, lambie-pie," Juno said. "We don't want to confuse anyone. Let's keep it simple."

"Fine," huffed Hera.

"Iole," Crispus whispered, gazing at her terrified face. "I'm so sorry."

"Not your fault," Iole said stoically. Then a single tear streaked down her left cheek.

"Do you understand?" Juno asked the guards.

"We do," said one.

"Begone."

"Pandy!" Iole screamed. Then she and Crispus vanished, Iole's cry hanging in the air.

"That's it," mumbled Cloacina, so softly that Pandy barely caught it. "I'm done. They wanted to see the sewers . . . ?"

The moment that Iole and Crispus disappeared with the guards, Juno and Hera fell all over themselves with glee and congratulations. In that instant, Cloacina lowered her head just a touch and closed her eyes.

Within the space of a heartbeat, the draining bathwater began to gush with greater force out of the mouths and eyes of Cloacina's carved faces; such was the pressure that some of the faces actually exploded outward. Shards of rock flew all over the cavern as the water began to rise. Then the Cloaca Maxima quickly began to overflow. Desperately wanting to sleep, Pandy willed her eyes to stay open when she realized what was happening. A second later, the water level had risen by a full meter. Suddenly Juno and Hera grasped what was going on and both reared back to strike at Cloacina. Pandy summoned on reserves of strength completely unknown to her and leveled two fireballs directly at the eyes of both goddesses. Momentarily blinded, Juno and Hera fell back into the water.

Pandy turned to Cloacina to ask what she should do and was horrified to see that water was also pouring out of Cloacina's own mouth. Cloacina craned her head to look at Pandy, grinned—which nearly terrified Pandy out of her wits—and winked. Suddenly, Pandy was knocked off her feet and found herself floating in a rising sea of used bathwater.

And she couldn't keep her eyes open.

She only knew that she was floating swiftly but rather gently, bumping into something that felt like it might be Homer or Alcie, who were also floating. They were all bobbing in the water and heading toward the stone arch, which led to the Tiber.

The Tiber!

Pandy jerked awake for only a moment. Time enough to see Juno and Hera flailing about.

"Can't swim!" said Hera, fighting to keep her head above water.

"Well, if you can't, then I can't!" Juno cried.

Then all was dark. Pandy had floated under the arch

and only seconds later was breathing sweet, fresh air as she headed down the mighty river that bisected Rome. Without warning, Morpheus appeared in her mind as she began to sleep again, a huge smile on his dark, beautiful face as he was about to speak. Then, he was gently shoved aside, rather surprised, as Cloacina stepped into view.

"Thanks, Morph. Just a few quick words, okay? Oh, that Morpheus; such a pal. Hi, Pandora!" she squealed. "First of all, real treat meeting you. Best of luck with your quest and all that. I've enchanted the water to hold up you and your pals until you hit the riverbank, so no worries about drowning. And Morpheus has promised to wake you all just before your heads go bonk on the stones alongside the water. Hopefully, you'll be able to get wherever you need to go before anyone catches you. So—probably won't be seeing you again—which is a shame 'cause I could have given you a sewer tour that very few mortals ever get. Ah, well. Anywho, just wanted to show you what you're missing now that you're out of my realm."

At once, a vision appeared: Cloacina's cavern at that precise moment. One tick on the sundial after Pandy had hit the Tiber: the water was rising, nearly covering everything, blurring the colored lights in the pools. Varius was gone. Everyone was gone. Only Cloacina herself remained standing. Submerged below her waist, water no longer pouring from her mouth, but her arms were stretched wide and she was laughing. And staring.

At the dam.

Two enormous blue objects, damming the flow as they slammed up against the stone arch of the Cloaca Maxima—unconscious, waterlogged, and too huge to fit through the main drain.

CHAPTER SIXTEEN
Prison

Iole stared up at the razor-thin slit high in the stone wall.

A single tree branch with three leaves; that was all she could see. Beyond that, nothing but blue sky.

A small bird suddenly landed on the very tip of the branch, cocked its head toward her, then flew away.

In her life before the quest, she hadn't thought much about people who were imprisoned, whether rightly or wrongly, or the state of mind someone might experience while confined to a small cell awaiting whatever fate was to befall them. Her life hadn't been focused on base ideas. She had been very concerned with justice, however, and the concept of fairness: lofty notions of man's humane treatment of his fellow man. She'd simply assumed that more often than not, someone who was imprisoned was, naturally, guilty. Although her own brain was a mighty and powerful force, in her young age and naïveté, she hadn't fully comprehended that deviousness, trickery, and usury were also part of man's (and the gods') nature. She'd never even contemplated the possibility of herself being jailed for any reason or what it might be like. The whole notion was just ridiculous. Although now, gazing at the sliver of blue sky and recalling all her adventures with Pandy— *everything* they'd done and witnessed—how *could* she be surprised that this was where she'd ended up? It was just one more bend in the road, one more twist in their tale. Only this one was, for her, the last one. Now, Iole was experiencing something far beyond her wildest imaginings and there was only one word to describe it:

Apprehension.

They had left her alone in a cell, with no possible means of escape, to contemplate her end and it was the waiting that was the worst—the anticipation. She almost wished her own death was over and done with because the suspense created by her imagination was unbearable. It almost didn't matter what exactly was going to happen or how torturous her punishment would be; her mammoth brain was working overtime to make it worse.

Dirt.

Stones.

A pit. Light, then growing darkness. Dirt clogging her mouth, nose, eyes, and ears. Choking . . . no air . . . gasping . . . blackness . . . breathing dirt! Nothing but dirt . . . only dirt!

Without thinking, Iole yelped and grabbed at her throat. She turned quickly away from the sliver of blue sky and sank down the wall to the ground.

"Iole?" Crispus called softly from the next cell, his manacles clanking on the ground as he moved closer to the wall dividing them. "Iole? Are you okay?"

"Y-yes," she hiccoughed. "I'm fine, Crispus. Are you?"

"Well, since you asked, one of my wrist manacles is a little too tight, so that's not pleasant. There appears to be a great deal of scraped skin and a little blood, but other than that I seem to be holding up very well," he answered, then he paused. "Iole, I am so sorry."

"Crispus, that's the second time you've said that, and I'm afraid I must take issue with it. You did nothing, do you understand? *We* found *you* in the sewers. *We* enlisted *your* help. You were nothing but innocent, brave, and helpful last night. It is I who am sorry."

"Yes, I understand, but I'm still sorry," he said softly from the next cell. "I'm just sorry all of it turned out this way. I suppose I can tell you now. Now that it won't happen; ever since I met you, which I thought was many moons ago and now it turns out *that* was wrong. Anyway, ever since I thought I met you, I half hoped that—in thirty years, when you had finished with your service as a Vestal—that . . . uh, that you . . . and I . . . because I tell you on my honor, I would have waited. Of course that was before I found out that the entire Valerius household has been under an enchantment and you're actually not a Vestal but you *are* from another time and another country, which is very interesting but slightly inconvenient. And you're ten years older than I am, really; which would make me six in your world, which would just be weird."

Iole smiled in spite of herself.

"Anyway," he finished, "I had hopes."

"You're . . . not the only one."

"*Really*?" he cried.

"A maiden can dream, can't she?" Iole said quietly. "I never had any thoughts of anything of that sort until I saw you looking at me the other day. You see, that type of thing just doesn't happen to me. Perhaps it was just the berry juice on my lips . . . or the crocodile dung. Maybe you wouldn't be in such trouble now if I hadn't smeared crocodile dung on my cheeks."

"No dung," Crispus said. "Just you."

Suddenly there was a loud commotion in the front of the prison. A female voice yelled at someone, only to be barked at by the captain of the guards, who was then screamed at in return. Then there was a great deal of shouting as a group, including several guards in their clanking armor, approached Crispus's and Iole's cells. Iole could hear the captain's voice, furious as he stomped down the corridor.

"This is unheard of," he shouted. "Why would you need to measure, for Pluto's sake?"

All at once, Rufina appeared in front of Iole's cell. The smirk of delight and disgust on her face went nearly all the way around her head, which was now the size of a watermelon. She had gained so much weight from the enchanted bread that she spanned nearly the entire corridor, from one cell entrance all the way to another on the opposite wall.

"It doesn't matter, you buffoon, what you haven't *heard of* before," she said, her three chins hanging down below her neck, wobbling as she spoke. "My father is interrupting an entire feast tonight to punish this maiden and her male companion and he's tearing up a very expensive floor to do it. We only want to take out so many tiles. That's why we need precise measurements for both prisoners. Oh, slaves? Come here at once!"

Looking out between the thick iron bars, Iole saw some movement behind Rufina.

"Slaves!" she barked. "Don't add to your punishment; come here at once!"

Again, there was movement behind Rufina and a ruffling of her robes. Then came a few grunts and several sighs. Then Iole heard Alcie's muffled voice.

"A little help, please?" she said. "Excuse me, you . . . guard? Yes, would you just . . . just . . . oh, for Zeus's sake, shove!"

Someone gave a huge push and Rufina's waist rippled across the corridor, although her head didn't move. In that moment, Pandy and Alcie fought their way out from behind Rufina's enormous backside to the cell opening. It was only then that Iole realized that both of her friends were shackled at the ankles with chains so short they barely dragged on the ground.

"Oh, there you are," Rufina said, her body settling back into stillness. "What kept you? Never mind. Now, Daddy wants precision! I know how hard you two try to be precise and I know how difficult it is for you. Why, just this morning, you both were only moments away from stealing back onto your sleeping cots and not getting caught for the runaway slaves that you are. Except I am infinitely smarter than either of you and I was waiting. I knew, one night, you'd stay out too late and I wanted to be there to catch you. Still don't know why you were soaking wet, but the point is, you're not as precise as you thought you were, eh? Well, in addition to the death my father ordered for you tomorrow, you have to serve me today. And I want the exact number of cubits for each of your little friends so we don't rip any more of my dance floor than necessary. So go on, get to it!"

Pandy and Alcie waited while a guard unlocked Iole's cell door.

"And if you speak to the prisoner, I'll have your tongues removed right here," Rufina said.

Pandy and Alcie, who had both opened their mouths to say something low to Iole, shut them again and began to shuffle across the cell floor.

"My friends, Rufina?" Iole said, staring at the girl who was now the size of a Roman chariot. "You had to have my friends do this?"

"Well, what are friends for?" Rufina giggled. "And speaking of friends, you all might be interested to know what happened to Homer."

Alcie tensed. The last time she'd seen Homer was earlier that morning as they had all dragged themselves—and Varius, who was still without a mouth—out of the Tiber. Varius had run off in the direction of the nearest temple—dedicated to Jupiter, Pandy had said—probably to pray . . . silently. Homer had given Alcie a quick kiss on her cheek and had sped off toward

Caesar's insula as she and Pandy raced in the opposite direction.

"Just like you two fools," Rufina continued, "he didn't make it back in time either. And Caesar just happened to be home. The word around Rome this morning is that he was so upset at seeing his prized gladiator, whom he basically stole from my daddy, flaunting the rules right under his nose that he sent word to Daddy and together they came up with a two-part punishment that's a real doozy!"

"You don't say," said Iole, knowing that Alcie couldn't say a word.

"Oh, but I do! The second part is pretty standard. Homer is going to be put in the Forum with no weapon and three hungry lions on really, really long chains. There won't be enough left of him for the carrion crows!"

Iole looked at Alcie. If that was the second part . . .

"What's the first part of his punishment?"

"This was my idea and this is where it gets fun!" Rufina cried. "You know how tonight you're going to be buried alive?"

"That's the rumor," Iole said wryly, trying to keep the panic out of her voice.

"Well, once we figure out how many tiles to take up and how deep to make the pit, Homer is going to be the one doing the digging! Sort of keeps it within your little group—makes it more special, don't you think?"

Pandy and Alcie stopped mid-shuffle and just stared at Rufina.

"You are, without question, so inordinately psychotic," Iole said.

"Silence! Or I'll have you . . ."

"You'll have me what? Killed?"

Rufina was momentarily stopped mid-sentence.

"Melania just might have something to say about this, you know," Iole said.

"Oh, she does," Rufina laughed. "When she was told what you'd done, who you were found with, she denounced you to the household and went to the Temple of Vesta to pray for you. Reports have come back that she's also tearing her hair out and weeping, but I can't understand why."

Iole hung her head, realizing that Melania—the one adult she'd met in ages who'd taken an interest in her and cared for her—no longer believed in her. Iole felt as if she'd betrayed more than a sacred trust: it was almost as if she'd betrayed her own mother.

Silently, with only a look to each other now and then, Pandy and Alcie got on their knees—with great difficulty—and used their forearms to measure how many cubits to Iole's height.

"I count three and slightly more than one-half cubits," Pandy said, turning to another slave who was holding a writing tablet and stylus.

"Very good," said Rufina. "Now, the male."

Alcie gave Iole only a backward glance, but Pandy secretly managed to squeeze Iole's arm as she left the cell. They measured Crispus to be between three and three-quarters and four cubits. Then, as quickly as they arrived, they were gone. Only moments before, Pandy and Alcie had both been as close as they would ever be and now Iole knew she would never see them again. And that short time with them had been spent getting measured for her grave.

Iole sank to the ground in the middle of her cell and began to sob. In that instant, she had the one thought she'd never before entertained, the thought that betrayed everything her friendship with Pandy stood for: she wished she'd never come on the quest. The fact that Athens was probably still in ruins, that the world was changed for the worse with evils still in it, and that she was part of a tiny but heroic group so close to putting everything right . . . none of it mattered. Because in a matter of hours, she would be buried alive.

"Iole?" Crispus called. "Iole?"

But the girl who was always so practical, so logi-cal, and so thoughtful when Pandy and Alcie were beside themselves with anger, sadness, or frustration; the one of the three who was stoic, calm, and unflappable . . .

That girl was now beyond reach.

CHAPTER SEVENTEEN
Hera and Juno

Across the city, far from the gods' insula, Juno sat on a hard stone floor with Hera. Days earlier, when she realized that the other immortals were blatantly lying about Hera's whereabouts and she would have to take matters into her own hands, she swiftly—but quietly—annihilated a small family living peacefully on one floor of a modest insula and moved herself in. Watching the innocent family succumb to death, she told herself it was simply a necessary part of this whole ridiculous business of having to play host to the Greek immortals; that she and Hera would, of course, need their own little nest in order to finalize their plans to become the most powerful deities in the universe. Then she returned to the gods' crowded insula and watched, waited, and listened for the clues that would tell her where her counterpart was.

Now, after piecing Hera back together herself, then dealing with Varius, Cloacina, and "the brats" (she had adopted Hera's pet name for Pandora and her friends), Juno was pounding Hera on her back, forcing the rest of the sour bathwater out of Hera's lungs.

"Good girl," Juno said, giving Hera another hard slap across her broad shoulders. "Get it all up."

"I'm . . . I'm all right . . . all right. ALL RIGHT!" Hera choked out, finally catching Juno's hand before she could pound again. "Zeus's armpits! You have quite the arm there, my sister. You could be a discus thrower. I'm fine, thank you."

"Good," Juno said, leaning back against the wall. "Well, *that* was an adventure I don't want to repeat!"

"We won't have to," Hera said, her breath finally evening out. "When all this is over; when Lucius Valerius becomes ruler and your temples outnumber those of the other gods ten to one in Rome and mine populate every meter of Greece, you can move to Olympus with me. I'll have everyone else chained up in Tartarus by then, and we can have the run of the place. And no sewers!"

"Sounds delightful," Juno said, then she took out the new carved coin from the folds of her robes. "And now that you mention Valerius, let us make good use of his likeness. You know, I have to hand it to that artist,

211

Varius: he did this right on the gold. No wood carving, no mold; right on the coin itself."

"We didn't give him a choice," Hera replied. "And we made the metal pliable enough."

"But still," Juno said. "I'm feeling slightly generous all of a sudden. I'm going to do something for him."

"We let him live!" Hera cried.

"Oh, we can afford to be beneficent!" Juno countered, conjuring the image of Varius in the air. Then she snapped her fingers.

At that moment, just as he was trying to figure out how to feed himself a slice of bread through his nose, Varius's mouth reappeared on his face.

"You're a gracious goddess, Sister," said Hera.

"You know it," Juno smiled, then she snapped her fingers again and suddenly the one coin became thousands and Juno and Hera found themselves surrounded by mounds of glittering gold.

"Allow me," said Hera, flicking her wrists. Instantly, the gold was stuffed into dozens of cloth sacks, which promptly disappeared.

"You made the switch?" Juno asked.

"You have to ask?" Hera said.

"Apologies."

"Tonight, when Caesar distributes the gold to his senators, they will all hold up coins with the face of the most spineless, sappiest, most weak-gutted, greediest senator of all. And by Caesar's own decree, Valerius will have to be crowned ruler. Naturally, Caesar will revolt and be executed for treason; *then* our plans will really move forward. It's only a matter of time now."

"So," Hera said, getting to her big feet. "What are you going to wear?"

"I'm thinking red."

"The color of blood!"

"Precisely," said Juno.

"I'll join you. But I'm throwing in a little black—for the pit those two slaves will be buried in."

"Always so *creative*."

"I try."

CHAPTER EIGHTEEN
Delivery

"Give me something . . . *anything*," Varinia said softly. As angry as she was, she was also growing weary and couldn't bring herself to yell. "Anything to placate my husband."

Pandy and Alcie stood silent, each one wondering if the other was going to speak, then realizing neither had anything to say. Varinia sighed—her fortieth or so since her questioning began.

"In the years that you two have been with the household," she said, which of course immediately confused Pandy and Alcie until they remembered Hermes' enchantment, "I have come to think of you both as much more than simple servants. You two have become like daughters to me. Inasmuch as I do not have a daughter I would wish . . ."

Varinia paused and cleared her throat.

". . . on anyone, you two have always been a source of secret pride to me."

Pandy looked at this woman whom she had only known for several weeks, speaking about her in ways that should have thrilled her, and would have, if the woman had actually been her mother. Sibylline had never been proud of her daughter, at least not so that Pandy had noticed.

"But now," Varinia went on. "Now that you have tried to escape . . ."

"We didn't!" Pandy started.

"Hush!" Varinia said, holding up her hands for silence. "It doesn't matter, don't you see? You broke the rules and were caught. But if you can tell me anything that might mitigate your punishment, I may be able to save your lives. Normally, Lucius can't bear the sight of Rufina, but now she has his ear and tomorrow, after you have served at the feast tonight, you will be killed. Not simply punished as runaways usually are, but executed as a warning to all others. Tell me something I don't know. Were you all out together or were you two looking for Iole and Crispus?"

Pandy and Alcie looked at each other.

"You know you cannot save her," Varinia said gently. "But you can save yourselves. Were you looking for her?"

"No," Pandy said. "We were all together, but Crispus and Iole hardly even spoke to each other."

"Do you have any witnesses to that? Anything that would counter the testimony of the guards who say they found them on the street holding hands? Anyone who saw you?"

"Cloacina," Alcie said.

Varinia stared at Alcie in astonishment.

"Do you mock me?"

"No, mistress, no!" Pandy countered quickly. "She means that we just got so lost in the sewers trying to get back here before dawn. We were down there so long that if anyone could have seen us, it could only have been the goddess of the sewers. That's all."

"That's all."

"Then that's a pity," Varinia said. "I wish you *could* produce Cloacina, Alcestis. I do. I would welcome the stench if her words would clear you two of any wrongdoing. Now go and prepare for our guests. Try not to think too heavily upon tomorrow; I shall still speak to my husband, for all the good it will do. Go."

The walk back to their tiny room was more of a dodge, bob, and weave around the many carved wood, gold, and ivory cages that were propped up along every corridor on the upper floor. Cooing, squawking, growling, and howling filled the higher reaches of the house while the main room was undergoing final *final* preparations.

Pandy threw aside the flimsy privacy curtain as Alcie brushed by her and headed for the window.

"Can't you do something?" she asked, staring at the sliver of faraway green hills beyond the crush of the city buildings.

"What do you suggest?" Pandy called, having flopped on her cot.

"Burn it," Alcie said flatly, now gazing at two horse-drawn carts entering the courtyard. "We may not succeed, but we shouldn't let them win. Burn Rome."

The sharp, shrill calls of various birds rose from the corridor outside.

"Hounds of Hades," Pandy said, putting her hand to her temples. "There's no thinking about anything with *that* going on."

"Yeah," Alcie said, her eyes now focused like a hawk on the carts and their contents. Dido, on his chain in the garden, began to bark wildly in recognition. "Well, if you want your brain to really run out of your ears, c'mere."

Pandy was up and at the window in a flash.

"Gods, no . . ."

Below them, the first cart was brought to a stop as

two burly guards went to the back and poked at its passenger with two large poles. Pandy and Alcie heard Iole sob and try to stifle a scream as they herded her from the back of the cart toward the opening. Farther back, from the second cart, two other guards were roughly tossing Crispus to the ground.

"Iole!" Pandy called down.

Iole lifted her head and Pandy and Alcie could see the stains of her tears even at such a distance. She tried to smile and waved just a little. One guard saw her movements and took a whip to her ankles, which caused Pandy to grab at Alcie's arm. Dido pulled on his chain and its stake so hard, he was on the verge of tearing it out of the ground.

"Dido!" Pandy commanded, seeing the imminent danger. "Stay! Stay, boy!"

"Eyes on the ground, Vestal!"

Iole fell to the dirt and clutched at the stinging welts. Then she was pulled to her feet and prodded, along with Crispus, into a low-lying shed attached to the back of the house. She wasn't even permitted a last look over her shoulder.

"Like a criminal," Pandy mumbled, feeling her own tears well up in her eyes.

"That's what they think she is," Alcie said. "They weren't gonna bring her in on a bed of orchids."

"Yeah . . . yeah. Well, guess what, Alce? I think you had the right idea all along."

"I did? Which one?"

"We may not get home, we may not find Greed, and we may die in this garbage heap. But if they touch one hair on Iole's head, I personally will turn this place into such a fire pit, it will make Tartarus look like a field of wildflowers after a light rain."

Alcie looked at her friend and put her arm around Pandy's shoulders, already feeling Pandy's skin give off a slight warmth as she grew intent and agitated. Alcie hugged her tightly, seeing Pandy's determination.

"Good girl. Only this time, think of some way I can get in on the fun."

CHAPTER NINETEEN
Feast

"Water!" Lucius screamed at the top of his lungs. "Bring me water!"

"Lucius, lower your voice," Varinia said, noting the startled looks from her guests. "Why do you not drink wine like the rest of us? Even Caesar is enjoying himself!"

"If I wanted wine I would ask for it. If I wanted to be a sheep like the rest of you, I would look upon that fool as you do. I have called three times now. Where is that Pandora?"

"Probably thinking upon her fate to come when the sun rises," Varinia answered.

"WATER!"

Pandy raced in from the food-preparation room, trying not to slosh the water in Lucius's special pitcher as she hurriedly picked her way through the revelers.

"Here!" she called out. "Here, Senator."

She nearly tripped over the long pole tipped with ostrich feathers that Alcie was using to fan a large group seated off to one side. Then she stumbled again on the steps leading up to the dais where Lucius and Varinia sat at individual tables along with Caesar and several other important nobles. Lucius himself saved her from toppling off the dais and into the pit, which had already been partially dug in the middle of the tiled floor.

"I'm sorry, they're mixing all the water with the wine. It was hard to get to the well."

"I don't want excuses," Lucius growled. "Pour!"

Pandy filled the senator's cup to the brim and he began to gulp as if he were dying of thirst. But within moments, he spat all the water out, showering several people seated below, including one wearing a thin metal helmet plumed with small feathers. Zeus looked at Ares as the God of War began to rise and confront Lucius.

"Sit down now," Zeus said softly. "Just shake it off. You are not going to call attention to all of us by killing our host. Sit . . . *down*."

Ares fell back into his seat and rolled his yellow eyes as Aphrodite patted his arm, which was considerably smaller than normal as all the gods had shrunk themselves to a more human size in order to blend in. Mars balled up a fist and held it out as a sign of solidarity.

Ares bumped it with his own and began eating his whole pheasant, bones included. All the gods, who were seated at several tables close together, glanced at one another.

"This water is foul!" Lucius yelled at Pandora, causing even Caesar to turn and look. "That is not my pitcher, you dull-witted wretch!"

Lucius reared back to strike Pandy but his arm was stopped by a firm grasp on his wrist.

"Lucius," Caesar said, standing over him. "Your guests are having a fine time. Why spoil it?"

Pandy seized the moment to speak very fast as she lowered her eyes and looked at the earthenware vessel in her hand—clearly the wrong one.

"I'm sorry, Senator," she said. "I just put yours down for a second. It's . . . it's so busy back there. It must have gotten mixed up."

Lucius yanked his hand out of Caesar's grasp and forced a smile at Caesar and then Pandora as Caesar returned to his seat.

"An easy mistake, slave," he said through gritted teeth. "Go and find my pitcher and return. Off with you."

Having seen the entire exchange, Hermes and Mercury shared a quick glance and arched a left brow.

Pandy glanced at Varinia, who had hung her head in shame, then turned to run back to the food-preparation room, but not before her eyes caught a glint of gold from a table close by. As she forced her feet to move, Pandy instantly recognized Aphrodite's enchanted girdle peeking out from under a plum-colored robe. Then she saw nearly the same girdle on Venus, sitting next to Aphrodite. She realized with a start that all the gods, both Greek and Roman, were sitting in the hall. They were smaller than usual, but there was no mistaking them as they gorged themselves on breads, honey paste, and game birds. Pandy caught Alcie's eye from across the room and tilted her head. Alcie looked where Pandy indicated, which happened to be the tables in front of her and, with a start, dropped her fan directly onto Minerva's head. Athena and Minerva both turned with a scowl at Alcie, who grabbed the fan, then smiled nervously and began fanning very fast.

Why were they here? To help? They knew *almost* everything, Pandy thought to herself, about the past, present, and future. What did they know that she didn't? The question remained unanswered as she slipped into the food-preparation room.

"Come on," Hermes said to Mercury, as he rose to follow Pandora.

"Right on your winged heels, Brother," Mercury said, tossing a piece of lamb back onto his platter and getting out of his seat.

Caesar rose from his oversize chair on the dais and, stepping over the pretty, young slave girls who had been placed in adoration at his feet, stood to address the guests. He took in for a moment the thousands of butterflies in the air above his head, the women about the hall playing with the monkeys and tiger cubs, and the black swans picking at the plates of those who had turned to gaze, in awe, at him.

"Honored nobles," he began. "Senators."

Then he raised his right hand in the air and swept it over the room.

"Romans!"

A cheer went up from all the guests. Caesar paused for effect, then lowered his hand and brought it to his heart.

"Friends."

"Oh, Pluto's teeth," mumbled Lucius.

"The time for celebration is drawing to an end," Caesar said, quieting a groan from the crowd with his hands. "And we must turn our focus to the great empire which is Rome. It is not enough to conquer countries and gain lands if we here at home are not mindful of all the citizens who make this city the finest, the noblest, the wisest, and the most powerful in all the world!"

Another louder cheer from the crowd. Even in her panic, as she hunted around the well for the lost pitcher, Pandy wondered what Caesar could be saying to get such a rise from the guests.

"I am going to further the highest seats of learning, build the most beautiful arenas for our games, and create the safest streets for our populace. And for this I shall rely on your continued cooperation, my friends. Because I cannot fulfill my plans, my hopes, and my dreams for Rome alone. I can do nothing alone. Alone, I *am* nothing."

"No! No!" shouted the crowd.

"Got that right," Lucius muttered.

"It is only by your grace and generosity that I occupy such a lofty position. One, I dare say, that is directly below that of the gods themselves."

Jupiter and Zeus looked at each other. Hera and Juno also exchanged a glance and a smile.

"But you have bestowed it upon me, unworthy though I am, and honor it I will. To that end, I have minted the aureus, as you all know. The coin that will always bear the likeness of he who leads Rome! And it is on this occasion that I shall give all the senators, to show my gratitude, a fair share of the empire's bounty."

At this point, two large slaves appeared from another room, each carrying a large tub full of bulging sacks. Lucius sat straight in his chair and stared at the tubs. Hera and Juno took a moment to squeeze each other's hands. The crowd's excitement was growing but Caesar held his hand high once again.

"Later, my friends! Later. Now, let the feasting and celebrating continue. I believe we have some special entertainments in store," Caesar said as resumed his seat. "Senator Valerius?"

Alcie stopped her fanning, letting the feathers settle onto Jupiter's platter, as she searched for any sign of Iole being brought in.

Lucius wasn't moving or speaking. It was as if he were deaf and blind to everything but the coins he knew were in those sacks. Finally, Varinia tugged on his robes.

"What?" he shot out.

"Rufina. Her dance," Varinia said.

"Oh . . . yes," Lucius said, rising. "Mighty Caesar and honored guests, my daughter shall now perform for you a dance."

"Interpretive," murmured Varinia.

"An interpretive dance," said Lucius.

He clapped his hands and Rufina, in a cloud of white silk, lumbered into the hall. Now, almost twice as wide as a horse, the sweat was beginning to form on her upper lip as she waddled across the floor to the dais where her parents sat with Caesar, whose eyes were wide with horror.

"Great Caesar . . . ," she huffed. "Hang on. Just a moment . . . need to catch my . . . breath. Okay. Well, *that* was a long walk!"

"Kill me please," Varinia said, under her breath.

"Now," Rufina went on, "it is my pleasure to perform for you my thoughts, various emotions, and ultimate sadness as I reflect, in dance and song."

"Song?" Caesar said, shaken out of his shock at the giant snowball with the tuft of black hair standing—assuming she *was* standing—in front of him.

"Yes, song . . . upon the final entertainment of the evening: the terrible but well-deserved punishment of Iole, the Vestal who has fallen from grace and brought shame to our household. Musicians, play!"

With that, the entire assemblage became riveted by the terrible spectacle of Rufina as she rolled around on the floor, gesticulating, panting, warbling, and stepping on her white silk scarves, tearing them to shreds.

Now in the food-preparation room, Pandy was knocking things over and onto the floor trying to find Lucius's special pitcher. Balbina hurried over with a tray of braised and candied apple slices.

"What's wrong, Pandora? Why are you destroying what's left of my little kingdom?"

"Wrong?" Pandy said. "Now that you mention it, everything."

"You must trust in the gods to see that all happens as it should," Balbina said.

"Yeah, well, that's sorta the problem. They're all here and they're not doing anything. Just sitting there."

"What are you talking about?"

"Nothing, Balbina. I have to find the master's water pitcher. Have you seen it?"

Just then, Pandy spotted another slave coming in from the well, holding the pitcher.

"Gotta go!" she said, heading across the room. But so many people were hurrying to and fro that she was knocked around and shoved aside for a time before she got to the area where the slaves were adding water to the wine. Pandy saw the slave set the pitcher down after emptying its contents into a wine vat. Immediately, Pandy picked it up again and turned to go to the well as the slave was holding a cup of newly watered wine out to Gallus, the burly household food taster.

"Taste," Pandy heard the girl say.

"Excellent," said Gallus. Then, unseen by Pandy, a look of shock crossed his face, as if he'd just seen the spirit of his long-dead mother. "Wait . . . give me some more."

"You've had enough," laughed the slave.

"I said *give me another cup, you stupid girl*," said Gallus in a tone that made Pandy stop; it was the same tone—exactly the same—that Lucius used with her on a regular basis. Pandy turned just in time to see Gallus strike the slave girl, sending her sprawling onto the floor; the tasting cup flying out of her hand. That's when time and motion suddenly slowed for Pandy, as if she had been meant to witness this scene in every detail all along. The people in the background almost seemed to stop moving completely. Oh-so-slowly, Gallus grabbed the cup in midair and plunged it into the wine vat. Then he brought out the cup and drank as if his life depended on it. Pandy watched as his throat bulged and contracted with each gulp.

Her mind racing but her movements trancelike, Pandy walked back toward the wine vat as the slave got up off the floor. Without looking at Gallus, the slave took hold of a nearby pitcher and began to fill it with wine. Roughly, Gallus knocked her down again.

"Nobody gets any of this wine," he said as time, to Pandy, sped up to normal.

Slaves began to stop what they were doing and stare.

"It's bad. It's poisoned," Gallus said.

Her curiosity was bubbling again to the surface and, without thinking, Pandy—who had never dared drink any water from Lucius Valerius's special pitcher—caught a droplet hanging off the lip of the pitcher in her hand, and brought it to her mouth.

Instantly she wanted another taste. It was just plain water, but she had to have more, and more, and *more*! She would do anything to get it; she would fill herself up like a water skin if she could. And beyond that, she wanted food and silks and money and comfort and things! She couldn't even name them all, but she wanted a lot of things. She hurried to the door leading outside to the well and had just stepped out into the night air when Hermes and Mercury blocked her path.

"Hello, Pandora," Hermes said.

"How are you feeling, maiden?" Mercury said.

"Out of my . . . ," Pandy began, not caring how fatally rude she was being.

"Oh, there's been a change in her, Brother," Mercury said.

"I would say definitely so," Hermes said, seeing the look in Pandy's eyes and the defiant way she clutched the pitcher. Quickly, he ran his finger around the rim then brought it up to his nose. He looked at Mercury and nodded.

"I'm thirsty. I want . . . ," Pandy started as she tried to edge her way around them to the well.

"I know what you want and why," Hermes said, stopping her with his little finger; although the gods were smaller in size, they still had all their strength and powers. Already Pandy felt the bruise blooming under her skin from where he'd only touched her.

"Ow."

"Deal with it and stay there," Hermes said, then his brows knitted together in deep thought for only an instant. "Pandora . . ."

"Look, you can stop me all day and all night long if you want, but I want more water," she whined, truly not caring who she was speaking to. "And I'm gonna get it. It's water. What's the big deal?

Hermes cleared his throat. "I have a message. From your father."

That one sentence instantly stopped her fidgeting and froze her to where she stood. Once again, she felt like she'd been hit in the face with a cooking stone. Hermes was the one god who had surprised her, threatened her, and been both generous and petty with her more than any of the others. Threats and pettiness aside, he'd looked out for her most of the time and was, more often than not, honest. But there was *no way* her father had gotten better; hearing her voice on the other end of a shell hadn't cured him, she was sure of that. And Hermes was a trickster—super smart and cunning, just like her dad. Her dad! Her *dad*? She didn't know whether to cry or jump for joy. So she began to yell.

"*You do not!*"

"Easy, maiden," cautioned Mercury.

"His message is this, Pandora: think."

"*Think?* What kind of message is that?"

"Think. Think about why you're here, what you seek, what you feel, and what you *hold*."

"My dad didn't say all . . ."

"*Think!*" Hermes shouted, which almost made her lose control of her bladder. Then she saw Hermes arch one eyebrow and, still aching for everything she wanted in the world—and more—it hit her like one of Zeus's thunderbolts.

It had been in her hands—her dirty, nail-bitten hands—the entire time!

Greed.

The pure, unadulterated source of Greed. The sixth evil that needed to go into the box. She didn't know if it was the pitcher itself or simply something inside that leached into ordinary liquid, turning it into an infection. It didn't matter. She'd held it in her fingers for weeks but had been too blind and off course to see it. Now, everything made sense. But she was rooted to the ground; her feet wanted to move her body in one direction and her mind was heading in another. The battle in her brain began to overwhelm her: find the box and put the evil inside, or get more of anything, everything.

Miserable and unable to move a muscle, she managed a stricken look to Hermes.

"Help me," she whispered.

Hermes' face softened.

"Together, Brother?" Mercury asked.

"It will take our combined powers to combat her contamination, yes," Hermes answered.

Mercury placed both hands on Hermes' arm as Hermes raised his other hand and slowly rotated his forefinger in midair. Slowly, Pandy felt herself turn; her feet lifted off the ground and, step by slow step, she walked back into the food-preparation area. Though the battle in her head still raged, she tried to focus on getting to the box.

"A message from her father?" she heard Mercury asking Hermes.

"It was the only thing she could hear," Hermes said. "She's infected; I hoped her 'greed' to see her family again would override her greed for everything else."

"Good call," said Mercury as the two gods disappeared.

Pandy fought her way back toward the wine vat.

"Stop saying that," Balbina was saying to Gallus. "It's *not* poisoned. You're still standing. Fill the pitchers."

Just as the taster was about to knock down Balbina

herself to prevent her from taking his precious wine, a sandy-haired youth came stomping into the room.

"Hilarius," Balbina said, turning from Gallus. "Why aren't you preparing your jokes? Varinia was very clear on this: 'The comic performs after Rufina to get the sourness out of everyone's mouths.' Rufina should be almost done!"

"Well, the order has changed now, hasn't it?" Hilarius spat. "Caesar became so insulted, so distressed at Rufina's wallowing white-hot mess, he cut her performance short and made it known to Valerius that he'd like to see something killed just to make himself feel better. So they've moved up the Vestal punishment. And he's gonna give out the gold."

Hilarius sighed. "Mother told me not to go into comedy. I'll be lucky if I get a five-minute set at the end!"

At the mention of Iole's punishment, Pandy's mind cleared for one instant and she stopped in the middle of the bustling room. Iole's death was imminent and she was now faced with an entirely different choice: save Iole *immediately* by any means possible without knowing what that might be, or get Greed back in the box, which might lessen the effect the evil was having on Lucius Valerius, thereby softening him in regard to Iole's punishment. But having Iole's execution called off was highly unlikely; Greed or not, the severe fate of a wayward Vestal was tradition, not to be dismissed. She watched a solid-gold platter, piled high with smoked eel, as it was carried out into the main hall; for a moment, she ached to grasp it, hold it, possess the beautiful, luminous metal. Then she physically slapped herself, hard, on her cheek, fighting against the lingering effects of Greed. She needed to put the pitcher someplace safe until she could get to her leather carrying pouch in her room. But where? Then the perfect solution flashed into her mind: the safest place of all would be in the hands of Valerius himself, and that would also give her the best vantage point from which to figure out how best to save Iole.

She began to move toward the entryway and suddenly realized her fingers were free to move. She wasn't holding onto anything. She looked down at the pitcher . . .

. . . but it was gone.

Frantically, she scoured the scene with her eyes just in time to see the pitcher, now full of tainted wine, disappear out of another entryway in the hands of a slave girl who'd conscientiously taken it from Pandy as she'd stood motionless in the middle of the room. All Pandy saw was the flash of Valerius's household crest on the pitcher and the bare back of the slave girl draped with strands of pink pearls.

Which she really, *reeeaaallly* wanted.

CHAPTER TWENTY

Chase

A scream from the main room—Iole's scream—jerked Pandy's attention back to the other entryway. Pandy could almost feel her brain growing twice its size in her own head as she focused on three things at once. She had to get to Iole, she had to get the pitcher, and she had to get word to Alcie and Homer. And she *had* to have those pearls.

No!

No, she didn't.

"Stop it," she reprimanded herself.

As she moved to follow the pitcher, another slave brushed by her on his way to the wine vat. Knowing that no more infected wine could be served, Pandy, without missing a step, turned her head and focused her firepower into the red liquid. Instantly, the wine exploded, vaporizing into a steam, which cooled as it hit the ceiling and fell in pink droplets to the floor. In the commotion that followed, she slipped from the room.

Attention was divided in the main hall. Those closest to the food-preparation room were trying to see what all the screaming was about and why the slaves coming out were stained pinkish red. Across the hall, Rufina was sobbing that she wanted to finish her dance as those about her assured her it wasn't necessary and that it was best to "leave Caesar wanting more!"

Guards were beginning to hand out sacks full of the aureus to the senators, one to each. In the middle of the floor, Homer, still shackled but able to use his hands, was standing with a crude shovel, being whipped to dig the burial pit even deeper. And in the far corner, two guards opened Iole's cage and began prying her clinging hands off the bars. As Pandy picked her way toward Alcie, her eyes were constantly shifting between Iole, the guards opening Crispus's cage farther back, the pink-pearled slave girl with the pitcher of Greed, and Homer digging in the middle of the room.

"Did you see them drag him in here?" Alcie said low through clenched teeth as Pandy stepped beside her. "Did you see them kick and shove my Homie?"

"Didn't see any of it," Pandy said. "I was too busy finding out where Greed was hiding."

"Well, I tried to kick and shove a few . . . *what*?"

"I found it, Alce," Pandy said. "It's here: in this room. But we've got problems."

"No! You don't say? I would never have guessed."

"Change in schedule," Pandy said into Alcie's ear. "They've moved up Iole's execution to, like, now. You've got to go and get the box from my pouch. Then find me in here, wherever I am."

"Done," said Alcie, dropping the fan, which landed at Zeus's feet. Jupiter and Zeus both watched as Alcie sped away and Pandy began to follow the pitcher.

"Where were you both just now?" asked Jupiter as Mercury and Hermes suddenly reappeared at the table.

"Getting a drink of water, Father," Mercury replied.

"That's right," Hermes said. "Needed a little break. Too much wine."

"Bite your tongue," said Bacchus, who then promptly fell asleep.

Hera and Juno, now both on the alert, began to rise.

"Oh, you're not going anywhere, my overbaked turtle-pie of love," Zeus said, forcing his wife to sit again.

"Neither are you, my honey-coated but somewhat-gristly piece of pork shoulder," said Jupiter, as Juno involuntarily plopped down at his side.

Pandy made her way toward Iole, having no idea what she was going to do. As she skirted the perimeter of the hall, she kept her eyes on the pitcher. Every time the slave poured a cup of wine, Pandy evaporated the liquid before the drinker even had a chance to take a tiny taste. With her focus on so many areas, though, she became slightly careless once or twice and actually exploded the cup itself. The slave girl was oblivious because of all the noise and most guests were too stunned or too pre-occupied to call her back. Several times, seeing Pandy as an empty-handed slave moving about the hall, guests gave her their empty plates or small bowls full of bones to take away, which she then absentmindedly handed off to guests at other tables.

Pandy was approaching Iole's cage when suddenly the guards were able to pry Iole's hands off the wooden bars and drag her out. Iole immediately lost all her fight and succumbed to terror as she looked wildly around the room. Slowly and with great ceremony, she was led through the deriding onlookers, past Pandy, and out toward the middle of the floor.

"P-Pandy," Iole stuttered.

But Pandy's mind was trying to prioritize and she stared back at Iole without really seeing her.

". . . and not just the Vestal," Pandy heard in the back-ground as Caesar called to the bloodthirsty crowd. "But her companion as well! See the justice of Rome meted out to those who deserve its wrath!"

Crispus, who had put up far less of a fight than Iole, was being ushered onto the floor. Pandy circled around the other side of the room as Iole was dragged to the pit. For a second, Iole was able to put her head against Homer's waist as a great sob arose from deep within her. Roughly she was yanked away and dropped, like a sack of meal, into the pit as the crowd cheered. Out of the corner of her eye, Pandy saw Melania standing solemnly in a corner, surrounded by several Vestals from other households, her face buried in her hands. Moments later the crowd went wild as Crispus landed next to Iole.

Pandy saw the pink-pearled slave girl making her way in front of the dais, close to the center of the action. Lucius also saw the slave as she crossed his line of vision and saw his special pitcher in her hands.

"You!" he cawed at the startled slave. "Here! Now!"

Just then, Alcie appeared in the entryway to the great hall, the box held tightly in her hands. Pandy motioned with her head and Alcie started making her way to Lucius.

Homer was standing still, the shovel hanging loosely in his hands, taking lash after lash from a guard's whip. Finally, seeing that he was hopelessly outnumbered and that the mob was beginning to throw things at him, he began to scoop the earth back into the pit, his lips trembling as he watched it land on Iole and

Crispus. Iole stared up at Homer, his toga now stained red, and tried to fling the dirt off her as fast as it rained down. Crispus could only mutter "I'm sorry" as pieces of dirt got caught in his hair and small stones pelted his face.

Pandy caught Homer's eye just as she turned her back on the scene and headed toward Lucius. It was time enough for Homer's face to register helplessness as Pandy hurried away.

The slave girl carrying the pitcher of polluted wine reached Lucius just as Alcie came up behind the dais with the box. Also at that precise moment, another slave handed Lucius his allotted bag filled with the gold aureus. For a second, Lucius didn't know which to grasp, his head whipping back and forth as if he were a young child given a choice between two favorite sweets. Pandy snatched an ordinary pitcher off the gods' table just as Venus went to pour a cup of wine and, coming up behind the pink-pearled slave, grabbed the Greed pitcher. She hid it behind her back as she brushed the slave girl aside and stepped in, smiling, to attend Lucius.

"Wine, Senator?"

Lucius locked one hand on the bag of coins and turned his head again toward the pitcher, reaching out for it with his other hand. Seeing that it was not his, but instead a plain, ordinary earthenware vessel, and then seeing Pandy holding it, smiling at him, her other hand behind her back . . . his mind snapped.

He leapt up in a blind rage and drew his knife from its sheath. It hissed through the air as he raised it up, but somehow his hand got caught in the many folds of his robes and the blade sliced clean though the bag of gold clutched in his other hand.

With Lucius's attention diverted as the gold coins began spilling out onto the floor, Pandy threw the infected pitcher to Alcie, who caught it in midair and shrunk back against the wall. Every fiber of her being told her to go to Pandy's side, but Alcie knew what was at stake if she lost the one thing they had come to Rome to find.

Lucius, knife in hand, was watching his portion of the gold bounce off the edge of the dais and skitter across the floor where it was instantly snatched up and pocketed by other guests. A few coins flew into the pit where Iole and Crispus were now nearly covered with dirt, causing Homer to pause as the supervising guard quickly stepped down, onto Crispus's head, to retrieve the loose gold.

"This is not Caesar!" came a shout over Pandy's shoulder. Pandy turned to see Hera and Juno, each holding a coin high for all to see.

"The official coin bears the likeness of Lucius!" cried Juno.

"Lucius shall lead Rome!" Hera said, a smile on her face until Zeus spanked her bottom so hard that she did a single backflip, landing in her chair with such a thud that she broke its wooden legs.

But the damage was done. A cry went up from the guests, who were becoming confused as to what was happening and who was actually going to be the imperator. Some were shouting for Lucius and some were still loyal to Caesar.

Lucius, his sanity gone and months of Greed still worming its way through his body, turned upon Caesar, who had been startled into an uncommon stillness, and raised his knife again. Pandy, without so much as a single thought for her own life, pushed Caesar aside before his own guards could even make a move.

And time slowed again.

She saw the profound insanity on Lucius's face, and *then* she saw the knife flying almost leisurely down toward her. She saw Alcie just starting to peer around the dais. Behind her somewhere, she thought she heard Homer scream above the roar of mob, and just as the knife point hit her upper chest, she saw Zeus's mouth drop open.

"Wow," she thought. "He's surprised. The king of the gods actually didn't foresee this."

Then she felt the most excruciating pain and saw the knife, buried to its hilt, just below her right shoulder. For the second time in two days, she felt herself lapsing into unconsciousness. This time, it was her body's way of protecting her mind from exploding with physical pain. But for reasons unknown, Pandy recalled the previous time she'd gone under; only hours before, in Cloacina's caverns beneath the city streets when exhaustion overtook her and she'd floated on a river of bathwater into the Tiber. From a tiny crevice in her brain, she recalled the funny, slightly disgusting chant that Crispus had used to call for help to the Goddess of the Sewers.

> *"Soft, yet cohesive let our offerings flow,*
> *Not rashly swift nor insolently slow.*
> *Accept our offerings as all we have to give,*
> *From earth, through us, and back again!*
> *And so, through you, we live!"*

"Gross," she thought, as she felt herself being lifted into the air. She was being carried off somewhere, and she couldn't open her eyes. Yet, in spite of everything, she tried to laugh at the icky singsong. "That's *so* gross."

She heard an ear-splitting crack, as if a thunderbolt had struck right in the middle of the hall; and then the screaming began. Pandy fought to open her eyes to see what had happened, but every muscle—even her eyelids—was paralyzed from the pain in her shoulder.

Then, as the world went black, she tried to remember all the pain she'd ever suffered on her quest; not the emotional distress or confusion, the self-chastising or frustration, but the real *pain* pain: being pierced by the tip of one the impaling poles in the Chamber of Despair, smacking hard into her uncle Atlas's chest as she hung from his giant nose hair, Aphrodite breaking her front left leg after Hermes had turned Pandy into a dog, and, in Persia, the genie Giondar throwing her so hard into a wall that she dislocated her left shoulder. None of it compared to this.

"Nope," Pandy thought, as every last nerve in her body flared up with a different kind of fire, one she couldn't control; her shock so extreme that she couldn't make a sound as the commotion around her faded into silence.

"Nope. This tops them all."

CHAPTER TWENTY-ONE

Down The...

In three swift motions, Homer landed a crippling body blow to his guard (who was standing slack-jawed at Lucius's attempt to stab Caesar), lifted Iole and Crispus out of the pit with both hands, then neatly deposited the guard into the pit in their place.

"What happened?" Iole yelled, trying to be heard above the din.

"The senator just tried to kill Caesar," Homer answered. "C'mon! I have to get you out of here before everyone turns on each other!"

"Wait!" Iole said. "Where's Pandy? Where's Alcie?"

"I don't know," Homer cried, straining to see over the crowd. "Everything happened so fast. When Lucius went for Caesar, a whole group of people stepped in and I couldn't see anything else. Iole, we have to get out of here now! I'll come back for them, but we have to move!"

"Not without Pandy and Alcie!"

"You take her," Crispus said to Homer, nearly toppling over as he was shoved aside by two guests searching for more of Lucius's lost gold. "I know my way around this house. I'll go find the others!"

"Find them, please. We'll meet just beyond the city wall on the easternmost road out of Rome," Iole said, giving Crispus a quick peck on his cheek, then turning toward the exit and the large front doors. She didn't see Crispus standing still and smiling for only a moment, his hand pressed against his face, before he disappeared into the fray.

Homer and Iole hadn't taken but two steps into the formal entry room, when suddenly there was an eardrum-bursting crack in the hall behind them that shook the entire house to its foundation.

Turning back, they saw a blinding flash of light as an enormous figure appeared on the dais, towering above those guards protectively huddled over Caesar and those wrestling with Lucius.

"Someone call me?" asked Cloacina, her high-pitched voice wailing like a siren.

At the sight of the sewer goddess, everyone flew into a greater panic and raced for the doors, which Cloacina had instantly shut by enchantment. Out in the entry room, blocked from getting back in, Homer and Iole tried hopelessly to pry the heavy doors apart.

"Cloacina," Jupiter said, calmly brushing the screaming guests aside as if they were the leaves of a large fern. "What brings you?"

"Well, certainly not any of you lot," she replied. "We all know I never get invited anywhere by *the family*."

"Oh, for my sake," Jupiter sighed as Zeus stepped beside him. "Yes, yes, we're horribly unfair. So, my question remains: what brings you?"

"The girl," Cloacina said, looking at the riot in the hall. "Pandora. She called to me. She chanted. Well, her mind chanted at any rate. She needs help of some kind. What is going *on* here?"

"Just your normal, average Roman feast," said Jupiter. "But the entertainment was disappointing and the food's gone, so we were just leaving, right, Brother?"

"Party does seem to be breaking up," said Zeus.

"Okay. Okay, okay. So, not only am I summoned by a mortal who doesn't have the manners to greet me . . . ," Cloacina humphed.

"Don't blame Pandora, Cloacina," Zeus interrupted. "She's been injured rather badly, I'm afraid. She's occupied in a mortal struggle at the moment."

"But you know what might be fun?" Jupiter said, looking around him. "If you quieted this thrall a little bit. Clear the house for Varinia. Her husband's probably going to be executed for attempted murder; the least we can do is help her clean up."

"Agreed," said Zeus.

"So, what? I'm invited basically to oust the revelers?" Cloacina choked. "Take away the trash? Toss the slop? What does a goddess have to do around here to get a little respect! Fine! Anything to get out of the cavern awhile. I'd advise you to get the family up off the floor or be prepared to get wet. I'm gonna keep this party going."

All the immortals immediately levitated themselves a meter off the ground.

Cloacina tossed her hair back and pointed directly into the pit, which immediately began to fill with water: foul, smelly water that topped off the pit and spilled over the rim, nearly drowning the guard who was trying to climb out. The water snaked its way over the floor and in a matter of moments everything and everyone was standing in a shallow but steadily deepening pool.

Then Cloacina closed her eyes and circled her forefingers in the air; gently at first, then building into a frenzy as she whipped her hands furiously.

"Here comes the fun part!" she cried, glancing through heavy lids at Jupiter and Zeus.

The water began to swirl around, faster and faster, creating a massive, sucking whirlpool. And the water continued to rise. Suddenly, the guard disappeared down into the funnel that had formed in the middle of the pit. Tiles were torn from the floor, chairs were dragged across the room with the force of the suction, platters with half-eaten hens sailed on top of the water only to be lost down the drain.

And of course . . . all the people.

One by one. Two by three by eight by twenty, they were all engulfed, uselessly swimming for their lives in the foul, putrid water, and sucked toward the gaping black hole.

Pandora was safely in the food-preparation room, both Zeus and Jupiter having seen to it that she was carried off by complaisant, unthinking slaves as soon as she had hit the ground and before the doors had shut. But Alcie, trying to follow her best friend, hadn't quite made it through the crush of people and had been swept off her feet with everyone else. Now, cursing herself for still not having learned to swim, she was dog-paddling with one hand by Zeus's feet, holding the pitcher high out of the water with the other, and fruit-swearing every phrase she could think of.

With a tiny motion of his finger, Zeus lifted her out of the whirlpool and raised her astonished face level with his.

"You promised you weren't going to use that kind of language anymore, maiden," he said.

"I . . . uh . . . did I?" Alcie chattered, never having

been so close to the King of the Gods. "Yes, Sky-Lord, I *did* but *again* I'm thinking I'm dying. So . . ."

"So nothing," Zeus said. "Go and help someone who probably is."

With that, Alcie felt herself flying over the maelstrom, clutching the pitcher tightly. Out of the corner of her eye, she saw Varinia, Caesar, Melania, the other Vestals, and most of the house slaves hovering in midair as the water swirled underneath. Alcie glanced to her left and saw Crispus also floating and moving through the air. Together, they reached the sealed doors to the food-preparation room which opened for only a moment as the pair flew through, then closed up tight again. Alcie was deposited at Pandy's side as she lay on a blanket in a corner. She heard a snarl coming from another corner and Alcie saw that Lucius had also escaped the whirlpool and was now being held down by four guards, who had knives poised over his body.

Alcie crawled over and put her hand on Pandy's arm as Balbina smoothed the hair back from Pandy's face, now ashen and cool. They stared at the knife still protruding from her shoulder.

"Pandy," Alcie said, hunching over. "Pandy? Balbina, can she hear me? We've . . . we've got to get the knife out."

"I won't be responsible," Balbina said, shaking her

head and looking at Alcie. "I have no skill here. I could take that thing out and it might mean the end of her."

"But if we don't take it out, she'll die!"

Two shadows loomed large in the lamplight.

"She'd probably die either way," said a deep voice.

"Leave it in, risk the body going into shock and possible infection," said a second voice, similar to the first.

Alcie and Balbina turned and stared up at Apollo and Phoebus Apollo.

"Take it out and you might never be able to staunch the wound," said Phoebus. "Yes, it's a rather ghastly, but somewhat ordinary, mortal wound. Normally, I'd say hopeless."

"And normally, I would agree with you," Apollo said. "If this were an ordinary mortal."

"What do you mean?" asked Alcie.

"Maiden, rotund kitchen slave, concerned onlookers," said Apollo. "If you please . . ."

Apollo and Phoebus slapped each other's hands high in the air.

"Stand back and be amazed!"

CHAPTER TWENTY-TWO
A Chat

"Hellooooo?"

Pandy heard, or thought she heard, a soft call; an owl perhaps. An "ooooooo" from somewhere far away in the night.

"Hellooooo?"

There it was again. She couldn't tell if her eyes were closed or open and she was in complete darkness.

"Pandora? C'mon, honey. Hellooooo?"

"Hello?" she whispered.

"There's the girl! I knew I hadn't taken you too far under."

Wherever she was, the inky blackness all around her began to lighten a bit and Pandy saw a shape materialize out of the shadows.

"Hello, Pandora," said Morpheus softly, drawing near to her. "I must say, you had me frightened there for a moment."

Two oil lamps hanging from high above suddenly illuminated and Pandy realized she was lying on a soft couch in a large cave. She looked up at Morpheus's beautiful, dark face; his blindingly white, perfect smile comforting her.

"Why?" she asked, genuinely intrigued. "Why were you frightened?"

"Because your wound is so severe and the pain is so great for someone of your tender years, the line between unconsciousness and death is extremely fine. I thought I might have crossed it."

Suddenly Pandy remembered the knife. She quickly looked at her right shoulder, expecting to see the hilt still embedded in her flesh. She was more than a little surprised to see . . . nothing.

Her shoulder was gone.

The bottom half of her arm was there as was the rest of her, fully functional, but the wide strap of her toga that ran from her neck to her upper arm was hanging limp in the air.

"Huh?"

"Oh, you won't see it again until they decide if they can save you or not," said Morpheus. "They sent you to me while they talk the matter over, the golden boys. There was no need for you to be conscious, so you're here with me. We're waiting for good news! Or not. So to speak."

"Golden boys?"

"Apollo and Phoebus Apollo. You have the best physicians in the world working on you. Although, and I probably shouldn't tell you this, they're having some trouble."

"With me?" Pandy asked with a start. "Why? What?"

"Seems they can't stem the flow of blood."

"Why not?"

"Well, and I probably shouldn't tell you this but . . . it's you."

"Huh? Me?"

"Yep. You're putting up a fight. That's why they're having such a time of it. That's why I thought perhaps I'd crossed the line. There's a part of you that really wants to cross the river Styx. A part that doesn't want to go back to the living world."

"No!"

"Oh, it's nothing you're conscious of—not topside, anyway. Not when you're up above being the go-getter we've all come to know and love. But here's this chance to stop running and searching and chasing, and simply settle down, and there's a large part of you that wants to simply rest now."

"Okay, not to be disrespectful or anything, but first . . ."

"Fire away."

"I'm semi-immortal, so I can't die."

"True. But the mortal part of you could take the immortal part and camp out in the Elysian Fields for a while. I mean, you can't separate the immortal part of you, so where you go when the mortal part of you finally dies, it will go too. Not necessarily a bad thing. Or you could morph into something else. Many options."

"And second . . ."

"Lemme have it."

Pandy was about to violently protest any suggestion that she wanted to stop hurrying all over the world and quit the quest. She'd already come to the decision *not* to give up earlier, when she'd shaken herself out of her stupor. Now, there was a question about it? Some renegade part of her brain suddenly wanted to quit and was helping to send her to Hades?

Of course . . .

Of course, if she were hurt. That is to say, through no fault of her own. If she were killed; well then, naturally, she'd have to give up. But it wouldn't be *her* doing. No one could blame her. She hadn't foreseen Lucius's knife piercing her flesh. No one could *blame* . . .

Then she realized everything Morpheus was saying was absolutely true.

"And second, you're right. I'm tired."

"Of course."

"And this would be . . . it would be easy."

"Extremely."

"Not my fault."

"Not in the slightest," Morpheus agreed.

"No one could say I didn't try."

"Artemis's delicate underclothes, how you tried!"

"I got most of them in the box," Pandy said softly.

"That you did," Morpheus said, nodding.

"I did a lot."

"Certainly."

Morpheus was silent as Pandy stared up at the oil lamps.

"Of course, *most* doesn't really count," Morpheus said at last. "Even with one or two evils loose; especially the last one, whew! Tough times ahead. But you did your best and that's all that matters."

"That's right," Pandy said. "That's right."

She stared off into the deep recesses of the cave. Morpheus picked at a piece of lint on his black and silver cloak.

There was no option, of course, no choice, and she knew it. In fact, she realized fully that all the sulking, brooding, and thinking she'd done about finding a way out of finishing had only wasted what precious little time she had left.

"Most doesn't count," she whispered to herself.

"I need to go back," she said aloud, looking at

Morpheus, who suddenly smiled so big that Pandy thought his face would crack in two.

"Let's hope we can get you there."

The next instant, Pandy's shoulder materialized, the knife wound still bleeding profusely. And with it came the unbearable pain. Pandy was so shocked at the magnitude of it that she gasped, then held her breath, as if by not breathing she could somehow stop the agony. She braced herself to scream.

Then she felt a hand—large, gentle, and unseen—on her shoulder. The pain stopped, and so did the blood.

"Bye," Morpheus said.

Pandy had enough time to meet his eyes and see his smile.

Then she blacked out.

CHAPTER TWENTY-THREE

Rufina. Again.

Even in the formal entry room, Iole and Homer could hear the screams, muffled as the screamers were fed into in the whirlpool. They heard bones snapping as bodies crashed into tables, broken bits of the dais, and each other. They looked down at their feet and saw dirty water seeping slowly from underneath the doors.

"Pandy! Homer, help me! Alcie's in there, Homer—and Crispus!" Iole gasped, trying to peer through a crack, any crack in the door. Nothing.

"Iole, come on," Homer said, gently pulling her away. "There's no helping anyone in that room now. Even your big brain can't break the enchantment of a goddess. We can't get in."

Iole twisted in Homer's strong grip, angling to get back to the doors.

"Iole! Look at me! The windows in that room were

high, but maybe they got through them somehow. Maybe Alcie climbed. . . . there was a door to the food-preparation room, right? We just have to hope that they got out."

"Oh, yes!" came a mocking voice from the stairway. *"Let's just hope they got out!"*

Iole and Homer turned to see Rufina, huffing and clutching at the railing as she tottered, unable to see the steps, on her way down.

"Rufina," Homer called. "Is there any other way to get into that room?"

"Shut up, slave," she panted.

"Rufina, *your parents* are in there and something really horrible is happening," Homer went on, trying to appeal to her love for her family. "You have to help!"

"I don't have to do *anything*. And I couldn't care less about what's happening in that room, except that you, Vestal, obviously aren't yet buried under it! When I am through with you both, you're going to *wish* you were in there, no matter what's going on. I am going to see to it that you are tormented, stretched, ripped, rendered, and . . ."

Rufina descended the last step and gasped for breath.

"That's it," Iole said calmly. "Homer, put me on your shoulders."

"Where was I? Oh yes, branded, scoured, flayed . . ."

"Take me over to her," said Iole, and Homer walked across the floor.

". . . punctured, pierced, pounded . . ."

Iole drew her arm back and punched Rufina right in the face; breaking, from the sound of it, the blob that was her nose. As Rufina fell back, Iole clambered down off Homer and began kicking Rufina in the sides, rolling her around the entry room like a large ball while Rufina yelled her head off.

"All your fault! All! Your! *Fault!*" Iole spat out, her body heaving with the force of each kick.

"Iole!" Homer cried, holding her back from doing any serious damage to the incredibly obese girl. "Come on. Leave her. She can't get up and with a little luck no one will find her for days."

He turned Iole away, making certain she didn't see him give Rufina one last mighty kick that sent her rolling off into a small anteroom.

"Ow!" yelped Iole when Homer took her hand to lead her out of the house.

"What?"

"My thumb. The pain is excruciating."

"Your punching thumb?"

"Yes."

"Okay." Homer asked, "Remember when you hit

Rufina; did you have your thumb inside or outside of your fingers?"

"Inside."

"Let me see it," Homer said, gingerly examining Iole's swelling thumb. "It's broken. But hey, nice punch. Lotta blood."

"Oh, no," wailed Iole.

"Hah!" came Rufina's voice from the anteroom.

"It'll heal. I'll make you a splint. Next time, keep your thumb outside your fingers."

Just then, there was a crash and a shattering in the anteroom as a ceramic urn toppled off a pedestal and conked Rufina on her head.

"Ouuuuuuch," came Rufina's muffled voice, then the sound of her head bumping the floor as she passed out.

"I'll remember," Iole said, with a sad smile. "Next time."

"You never took me up on your Maiden Day present, did you?" Homer said, hurrying through the house and stepping out into the courtyard where he quickly untied Dido. "Ten free lessons in self-defense, including hacking and . . ."

He looked at Iole who was staring back at the house of Lucius Valerius; now quiet, as if everything and everyone had simply been washed away. Homer was silent.

"No, Homer, I haven't taken you up on your offer," Iole said, stifling a sob. "Maybe if I had, I could have put a stop to all this madness. Somehow."

"I don't think so, Iole. Not this," Homer said, lightly touching her shoulder. "It was still a nice punch, though. C'mon."

"Where are we going?" asked Iole.

"Your idea," Homer replied. "Outside the city wall on the eastern road out of Rome."

"That was when I thought there was a chance we'd all make it," Iole said, stopping short. "That was when I saw Alcie was still alive and Crispus—oh, Crispus—he never asked for any of this."

"Iole," said Homer, Dido at his side. "We're just gonna have to have a little faith."

CHAPTER TWENTY-FOUR
The Healing Touch

"I will say this, Cloacina," Jupiter laughed as he surveyed the hall. "You have style."

There was absolutely nothing left.

The tables, chairs, and pillows were gone. The floor lamps, gone. The tapestries and banners, gone. Plates, platters, and goblets . . . all gone. And there wasn't a living human to be seen. Two guests, a man and a woman, both still clutching several of the fake aureus, had gotten stuck behind a large pillar and had drowned there and then, but otherwise, the room was empty and silent.

And very wet.

And very clean.

"I do, don't I?" Cloacina chirped. "You should invite me out a little more often. Let the family get to know me better. Wouldn't always be turning their noses up at me if they were comfortable, you know? Or you could all come for an evening meal at my place! And then we could go for a moonlit sail on the Tiber. Sound fun?"

"Yes, my dear," Jupiter said. "A great deal of fun. Only we'll have to let all those waterlogged guests get a ways downriver."

"Hah," Zeus agreed. "I wouldn't want to be the first citizen to gaze at the Tiber tomorrow."

"I wouldn't worry about that," said Cloacina.

"What do you mean?" asked Jupiter.

"My realms are vast, Sky-Lords," said Cloacina. "I never said I was sending them into the Tiber."

"Okay," Jupiter said, with a pause to look at Zeus. "And now I'm scared."

"Right with you, Brother," Zeus said. "If you will forgive my hasty departure, Cloacina, I must check on someone. Jupiter, care to take a walk?"

The food-preparation room, one of largest in any private home in Rome, was now bursting with escapees from the whirlpool. Almost all were slaves, some from other houses who'd only accompanied their masters for the evening, good and obedient servants of Valerius, the weeping Vestals, Varinia, and many guards. The house had indeed been shaken off its foundation by Cloacina's "cleanup," and a large piece of stone had fallen from an upper floor and was now blocking the way out into the small garden where the well was. Many slaves were sitting on the wine-stained floor or standing still, confused, shaken, and clinging to each other. There was only a smattering of tears as most were still dumbstruck with the fearful sight they'd just witnessed—and survived.

The space in the room was made all the more cramped due to the fact that Caesar's guards were keeping him surrounded while they tried to move the large stone away from the door at the same time other guards were keeping everyone, even Varinia, at a distance from Lucius Valerius. And Alcie was snapping at everyone to stay back from Pandy, but that was proving difficult to accomplish; everyone close by wanted to see what the two golden-haired men were doing to the mortally wounded maiden.

Suddenly Zeus and Jupiter pushed their way through the crowd, followed by most of the other immortals. The humans in the room were squished up against the walls; some were nearly trampled.

"Why does she still lie on ground, son?" Zeus asked Apollo as he stared at Pandy. She was now beyond pale, blood flowing freely from the wound in her shoulder, piles of soaked rags off to the side.

"We cannot stem the flow of blood," answered Apollo.

"Her wound was serious to be certain, Phoebus," said Jupiter. "But your skill outweighs any mortal weapon."

"Phoebus?" shrieked a woman standing close by.

"Great Jupiter," answered Phoebus. "We have tried every method we know. We have removed the blade but the wound will not staunch. It's as if something is interfering with our power."

"Jupiter? Jupiter! Hey, everyone, look, it's Jupiter and Phoebus," a man crushed against a nearby wall began to shout.

"I always thought Jupiter was bigger!"

"No . . . no! It's *him*! I'd recognize that face anywhere!"

"I think I see Venus, and someone who looks just like her!" said another man.

"You have all the powers attendant upon the god of healing, my son," said Zeus to Apollo. "This is not . . ."

Zeus turned to see nearly the entire room on their knees in front of him. All the gods—only Hera and Juno were missing—found dozens of mortals at their feet.

"Oh, heavens," Jupiter sighed, turning. "Game's up."

"Mighty Jupiter," began one man, wringing his hands. "I have been out of a job for seven moons now; is there anything you can . . ."

"Great Phoebus," cried a woman. "My son has been turned away from the medical academy. Do you think you could put in a good word?"

"Minerva! Oh, wise Minerva! My wife spends money like a sailor with one night ashore. Would you curse her for me?"

"Venus? Oh, then you must be Aphrodite! I have a pimple on my . . ."

"Bacchus! Would you sign my toga?"

Jupiter looked at Zeus.

"Were all these people in here when we walked in?" he asked sideways out of his mouth, trying to maintain a beneficent smile.

"I don't know. I tend not to really notice mortals up close."

"Okay, citizens, show's over," said Jupiter. "Nothing to see here. Move along."

"They can't move, Father," said Mars. "Big stone blocking the exit."

"Not anymore," Zeus said with a flick of his forefinger, sending the stone toppling. "Everyone who needs to stay, stay. The rest, begone."

No one moved. Only Pandy moaned slightly in her unconsciousness and that was all Zeus needed. With one glance over the room, he took in those with a reason to remain. With a nod of his head, everyone else vanished.

"Tell me you didn't pull a 'Cloacina' and send those slaves down a drain to nowhere," Jupiter said.

"They're right outside and out of the way," said Zeus. "Now, sons, what keeps you from healing this maiden?"

"Might be me," came a deep voice from a shadowy corner.

"And me."

"Buster!" cried Persephone. "It's my big Buster!"

"Hi, honey-cake," Hades said, grabbing his wife and giving her a whirl.

"Miss me, lambkins?" said Pluto, stepping forward and planting a kiss on Proserpine.

"And *how!*" she said.

"Oh, well, *that's* just terrific," said Phoebus. "No wonder we couldn't get anything done. No offense, Uncle Pluto, but your natural death-waves are really wrecking the good vibrations we're sending out."

"Faaaather," whined Apollo. "We want to heal her. Make them *stop!*"

"We're not here for the girl, nephew," said Pluto.

"Nope," said Hades. "She's all yours, you hacks. It's just that it's getting chilly up here in the mortal world, which means winter is coming on. We need our snuggle-bunnies to keep us warm. Remember, Persephy . . . it's your promise. Six moons up here and six moons with me."

"Oh, Buster-boo," said Persephone. "I can't wait, you

know that! Let me just say good-bye, then you and I can get outta here!"

"That go for us too, squash-blossom?" said Pluto to Proserpine.

"Double, my big, lord-of-the-dead fuzzy-wuzzy."

"Okay. Seriously?" said Aphrodite. "You two talk like that for six months? *Seriously*?"

"Yep," said Alcie softly.

"I'm the goddess of love and that's making even me sick."

"Wow," snorted Apollo. "I am so glad you don't show up at more family reunions, Uncle."

"You know nothing about how to keep the flames of love alive, you silly boy," said Hades to Apollo. "All you do is get ladies turned into laurel trees and such. Come on, P."

"Hang on, *H* to the *A* to the *D* . . . ," Persephone said, already on the move.

She glided over to Alcie and kissed her on the forehead. Then she took Proserpine's arm, and the two goddesses went to Pandy. Persephone gently placed her hand directly on the still-flowing wound. Immediately, the blood slowed to a trickle and Pandy, with a great shudder and gasp, opened her eyes.

"How did you . . . ?" asked Phoebus.

"What gives?" said Apollo.

"Silly boys," said Persephone. "We're the goddesses of springtime. Which means we have the ability to stimulate life where there appears to be none. To bring hope in the darkness. To revive that which is thought to be dead."

"I know," said Proserpine.

"I *know!*" said Persephone.

"Isn't that right, Pluty-wooty?" giggled Proserpine.

"As rain," said Pluto, pinching her playfully.

"Pandora's body had just shut down, that's all," said Persephone. "And her spirit was in tremendous confusion. I don't wonder why, with everything this maiden has been through. Neither Hades nor Pluto was wrecking your vibes, uncles. It was Pandora herself, on the brink of a very im-por-*tant* decision. She didn't even really need our help, but if any goddesses can stir up a positive outlook it's Proserpine and I. It didn't take potions or spells; just a little breath of spring. A little revival. Now, Uncle, you may handle all the silly topical stuff. Okay, we're off!"

"This was fun!" said Proserpine.

"I know!"

"I KNOW!"

Hades, Persephone, Pluto, and Proserpine disappeared in a flash of black smoke and a shower of white rose petals.

"Topical stuff!" said Apollo.

"Quiet and attend to the maiden," said Zeus, as Pandy began to stir. "Immortals, away! Pandora has a few things to accomplish after she fully wakes and we should not distract her further with our presence. We have a few things to do ourselves, don't you agree, Brother?"

"I do," said Jupiter. "And first on the list . . ."

He waved his hand and the entire room, except Alcie, Crispus, Varinia, Lucius, Caesar, and their guards, fell into a deep sleep.

"When they wake, they'll only remember a grand feast with some exceptionally bad entertainment."

Zeus then waved his hand in a wide arc in front of his body.

"Brother?" asked Jupiter.

"Something we should never have let get out of hand in the first place," Zeus said, crossing the room and reaching down to pluck a stolen aureus from the pocket of a quivering guard. Tossing it to Jupiter, Jupiter could see the likeness of Caesar engraved in the gold.

"Back to the original," Zeus said. "Clear up that mess once and for all."

Lucius groaned and slumped where he stood.

"Sorry, Senator," Zeus said. "No ruler of Rome for you. You're just going to have to content yourself with being an extremely powerful personage in one of the greatest societies in the world. Deal with it, my good man."

"Which puts me in mind of two lovely bovine-figured goddesses we should seek out," said Jupiter.

"Hera?" called Zeus. "My precocious little pork patty! I'd like a word, please!"

"Come to me, my gorgeous gobbling goat," Jupiter said loudly. "Juno? Don't make me come to you. Won't turn out well."

Neither Juno nor Hera appeared.

"Good," said Zeus. "I'm in the mood to hunt some big game."

With that, the Sky-Lords vanished.

CHAPTER TWENTY-FIVE

Greed

Pandy tried to sit up, but the pain was still so great that she fell back again, beads of sweat breaking out on her forehead.

"Morpheus," she mumbled, closing her eyes. "Take me back."

"Now, now," his voice called from somewhere deep in her mind. "We had a lovely visit, but you made your choice and it was the right one."

"But it hurts," she whispered. "It hurts *so* much."

"You can't make an oatie cake without cracking a few eggs," she heard him say. Then his laughter faded into silence and she opened her eyes.

"I don't even know what that *means*," she said absently, staring up at the ceiling. Then Alcie's face loomed over her and behind Alcie, Apollo, and Phoebus.

"Pandy?" Alcie said. "Pandy, can you hear me?"

"Yeah," she replied. "I can. I can hear you."

"Oh, blessed Athena, blessed Zeus, blessed everyone else who I can't remember right now. I thought you were gone. I mean really, really gone."

"I was," Pandy said, trying again to sit only this time Apollo and Phoebus moved to help her. "I *was* gone." Pandy looked down and saw that her injured shoulder was heavily bandaged and her arm was in a sling. Immediately, she thought of the Eye of Horus; she didn't even know where it was and couldn't remember the last time she'd seen it.

"Are you thinking of this?" Apollo said, holding up the amulet.

"I was," Pandy said, looking at the two identical gods. "I am, Great . . . uh . . ."

"Apollo."

"Thank you," she said reaching for the Eye. "Where did you find it?"

"Who cares?" said Phoebus. "I think one of your little friends had it in her pouch—or maybe it was you. No matter. I wouldn't give you a drachma for it; silly Egyptian hoop-de-doo. It won't help you really."

"We have something much better for you," said Apollo.

"All you need to do is apply a special poultice three times a day under clean bandages; we've added supplies of both to your pouch. In a few weeks, you'll never know the knife had been there."

"Thank you," said Pandy, gently taking the amulet from Apollo. "But I'd like to hang on to this, if you don't mind."

"Tell me she's not being ungrateful, Brother," said Apollo, closing his eyes and turning his head dramatically. "Tell me she's not rejecting the medical advice of the two greatest physicians in the universe."

"I wish I could." Phoebus sighed. "I wish I could."

"No!" Pandy said. "I'll do exactly as you suggest. I'll follow your instructions, I promise. I just want to hold on to this as a—a reminder of everything that's happened. You know . . ."

She was about to tell them of the all the healing the little amulet had done in the past months, but quickly decided against it. Instead, she casually slipped it around her neck and instantly felt the pain in her shoulder subside.

"Thank you, mighty gods," she said. "Thank you for bringing me back. Thank you for saving me."

"Oh, apparently *we* didn't actually," said Phoebus in a mocking tone. "Apparently, our little nieces, Persephone and Proser . . ."

"Ahem!" coughed Apollo. "Hmmm . . . ahemmm. You're very welcome, Pandora. You might remember us especially when next you're trying to decide who to worship first on a feast day."

"I will," she answered. "I will."

"Then let us be off, Brother," Apollo said, rising. "I feel the need to heal some more. Let's see if there's anyone who's lost a limb or two."

"Sounds grand!" said Phoebus. "Maybe a complete dismemberment! After all, this was one wild night."

The gods vanished in a shower of gold dust and Pandy looked up to find Alcie sitting next to her on the floor.

"Hi," Alcie said.

"*Hi.*" Pandy sighed. She went to hug Alcie, but the residual pain in her arm caused her to wince.

"Easy."

"What did I miss?" Pandy asked.

"Too much to tell you now."

"Iole? Homer?"

"Don't know. The last I saw, Homer was scoopin' dirt into the pit. Then you handed the pitcher to me, then you got . . ."

"*Greed!*" Pandy exclaimed. "What happened to it? Where is it?"

"Right here," Alcie said, pulling the pitcher from where she'd been hiding it with her cloak against the wall. "And I have the box right here."

"Give me that pitcher!" screamed Lucius Valerius

from across the room. "Give it to me or I will see you both devoured by lions!"

Alcie filled her lungs with air as she turned.

"*Shut up!*"

Varinia gasped, but Lucius closed his mouth.

"Alce!" said Pandora.

"I don't care. Respecting elders is one thing and normally I do, really, but this whole family just bugs me."

"Thank you for saving it," Pandy said, nodding toward the pitcher.

"It's box time!"

"Got that right," Pandy said, moving to slide the pin out of the lock on the box. "Then we have to find Iole and—ow! Ow . . . okay. Okay. Alcie, I can't move fast enough. Not fast enough to toss it in without anything else escaping. I can't even get the pin out. There's still a lot of pain. Ow! This is worse than when Giondar dislocated my left shoulder. Much worse. You're gonna have to put Greed in the box."

"Uh. . . . Uh-huh, yes. And would that be . . . by myself?"

"You can do it."

"I can?"

"Alcie," Pandy said, looking straight into her friend's eyes. "I trust you more than anyone I know. You can do it."

Alcie sighed deeply and Pandy could tell her friend was terribly nervous.

"You got this," Pandy said.

"Yeah," Alcie smiled quickly. "Well, sure. Yeah."

Then she slid the box in front of her and, with a little side coaching from Pandy, withdrew the hairpin and flipped the clasp. She grabbed the pitcher and went to open the lid, then she paused.

"You trust *me* more than Iole?"

"Hermes' helmet! Put. The. Evil . . . inthebox," Pandy said through gritted teeth.

"Right."

In one fluid motion, Alcie raised the lid and stuck the pitcher inside. But even though the pitcher immediately began to bubble and steam away, it was still too large for the lid to close. Within moments, Pandy and Alcie saw a red streak of thick smoke snaking it's way from the back toward the front. Then a brown streak. Pandy began pounding on the lid of the box with her good arm, sending white-hot pain into her upper-right side as she tried to force the pitcher to sizzle away faster, but to no avail. Alcie began blowing on the ugly streaks of smoke, now four of them, trying to drive them back, but they were moving steadily toward the opening.

In her mind, Pandy saw all the misery, the frustration, the loss, the death as well as the triumphs, the joys, the bonds, and the love they'd experienced in the last several moons—in short, all their hard work—evaporate as the streaks began to rise into the air. It was all going to be for nothing, because everything was getting out again. Evil was being loosed on the world once more and she didn't even have the strength to scream.

Out of nowhere, a glint caught her eye. Then two familiar forms came into focus just before Pandy's eyes were diverted by a spinning whirl of metal seemingly heading straight at her. In the next second, before she or Alcie had a chance to breathe, the adamant net dropped with precision and settled over the rising streaks of smoke, pushing them back down toward the box. Suddenly, a sandaled foot was stomping on the evils.

"A little help here?" said Iole, kicking the net.

"Hah!" said Alcie staring up at Iole then shaking off her momentary shock. She began pushing the evils back inside the box with the flat of her hand as Pandy feebly pounded on the top trying to force the lid down. Homer joined Pandy and pressed down hard, but they stopped when it sounded like the wooden top was starting to crack.

Finally, the pitcher sizzled away enough that Alcie was able to close the lid, flip the clasp over the lock, and slide the hairpin through once more. Homer and Iole sunk to the floor beside Alcie and Pandy. Everyone was breathing as if their lungs were losing more air than they were taking in, and no one said anything for ages. Alcie gently slid her hand over Homer's.

"Why are you breathing hard, Homie?" she asked, her eyes closed, but a smile on her lips. "I mean, it's not like you were in a fight or anything."

"Scared," Homer said.

Suddenly, everyone heard a thud against the far wall as Lucius Valerius slid down onto the floor. His body was completely limp and droplets of Greed-sweat began beading up and pouring off his skin.

"That's gonna be some headache," said Alcie.

"May I be the first to say, Homer," said Iole, her breath coming a little more evenly. "Painstakingly perfect throw of the net."

"You know it," Pandy agreed. "Nice going, everyone. Alcie, you were fantastic!"

"Yep," Alcie said, opening her eyes. "Well, it was easy. I was confident, y'know? Now that I know you trust me more than—"

"*Iole!*" Pandy cut in, glaring at Alcie who just grinned. "How did you find us?"

"There are three entryways into that room," Iole said, pointing toward the great hall. "One was sealed. Two originate from this locale. We knew we had to start here."

"We were by the stairs when we saw the flash and then the doors closed," said Homer. "We saw water seeping from the room. We heard screaming. What happened in there?"

"We'll fill you in on all the gory details later," Alcie said.

"How did you know to get all our stuff?" asked Pandy, seeing her and Alcie's pouches slung around Homer's neck.

"We were on our way out of town," Homer answered. "I made Iole come with me, and Crispus promised to get you two."

"Crispus!" Iole said, looking around. "Is he all right?"

"He was a while ago," Alcie said. "He floated in here with me. We'll find him. Go on, Homie."

"Anyway," Homer began.

"Anyway," Iole interrupted, "we were halfway along the eastern road out of the city when we both stopped at exactly the same moment, looked at each other, then raced back here."

"I was crazy to think I could just go and calmly wait outside the city for everyone to, like, show up," Homer said.

"We didn't know what was going on," Iole said. "But we knew we'd probably need to make a speedy departure. So I grabbed all our stuff and we came here."

"Good thing," Pandy said. "Okay, Homie, help me up please?"

"Hey!" squealed Alcie.

"I'm sorry," said Pandy. "Hom-*er*, will you help me up?"

"So," Alcie said, getting to her feet. "What now?"

"Now, we get out of this rat trap," Pandy said, motioning for Homer to drape her pouch across her good shoulder. "Would someone hand me the net and the box please?"

"Allow me to put these inside for you, Pandy," said Alcie. "Trusted friends should be able to do—ow!"

"Thank you very much," Pandy said, retracting her foot from having kicked Alcie in the shins. "And because I trust the two of you so much—as in equally— Iole, would you open my pouch and get out the map while Alcie puts the other stuff in and keeps quiet?"

"Certainly," Iole said, retrieving the blue bowl. "Alcie, did you concuss yourself? A possible head trauma? Because you're behaving even more oddly than normal."

"Just get Pandy's vial of tears, brainiac," said Alcie, rubbing her shins.

As Alcie held the glass bowl level and Homer poured in a little water, Iole uncorked the vial and added a single teardrop. As the concentric rings began to spin, Pandy looked at everyone. The rush of emotion caught her completely off guard.

"Guys? Do you realize," she said, as tears welled up in her eyes, "that this is the last time we'll ever have to do this?"

"Then I don't need to catch any more of those," said Iole, holding the vial at her side, watching a rivulet streak down Pandy's face.

"Nope," Pandy said. "No more."

"Six down," Alcie said, getting a little misty herself. "One to go."

At that instant, the spinning rings aligned and the familiar light illuminated three symbols; words, once again, in Greek.

"Fear," Alcie sighed. "The big one. Well, we knew it was coming."

"What does that say?" Iole asked. "The ring that tells us where we're going? Hold it steady, Alce, I can't read what . . ."

" 'Nine,' what?" said Alcie.

" 'Nine Days Down,' " Pandy replied, her voice catching slightly.

"Huh?" said Homer.

"Oh, no," said Iole.

"Oh, yes," retorted Pandy.

"*What?*" cried Alcie.

"Alcie, when I went up to Olympus it took nine days to get there, remember?"

"Well, I didn't exactly go *with* you, but yes I do recall."

"What's nine days in the opposite direction?" Pandy asked.

Alcie's eyes narrowed as she thought, then she gasped before throwing her head back with a laugh.

"We don't even know how to get there," Homer whispered.

"But," said Alcie. "But this is *fantastic*!"

"Her mind is officially gone," said Iole.

"Don't you get it?" Alcie said, picking Iole up and whirling her around. "They *love* me down there. I know people who know people! Persephone is, like, my *immortal* best friend. And I know my way around. I can give you a whole tour. We'll start with the food-preparation rooms. Snail custard! Wahoooooooooooo!"

"But we don't know how to get there without, y'know, *dying*," Homer said.

"Of course we do," said Iole. "The same way Orpheus did. He lived in Thrace. We'll go to Thrace."

"We'll follow the path he followed when he tried to bring his wife, Eurydice, back from the dead," Pandy agreed.

"It's a cave somewhere on the side of a mountain, or so I've read," Iole said.

"Underworld, here we come!" said Alcie.

"Weeks away, no matter how we go," Pandy said. "And how much time do we have left?"

"We have twenty-nine days," said Homer.

"And we know we're gonna be minus nine to begin with. That's already nine days less . . ."

"Less than . . . ," Alcie began.

". . . one full moon. Essentially, we'll have twenty days," Iole finished.

Pandy took the bowl out of Alcie's hands and tossed the contents. Wincing slightly, she stowed the map back in her pouch and strode toward the door to the garden.

"Then I guess we'd better get moving," she said, pausing only to gaze down at Caesar, who had tried to remain calm and observing during the events in the food-preparation room. "This man," she said, pointing to Valerius, "was under an enchantment when he tried to kill you. He has been under that enchantment and not . . . uh . . . Iole?"

"I'm going with blameworthy."

"Thank you, blameworthy for his behavior for the last few weeks. You will not punish him in any way or allow anyone else to punish him or anyone else in his household—except maybe his daughter. Is that clear?"

Caesar looked at Pandy evenly.

"Clear," he said sincerely. "You have my word."

"Groovy," said Pandy. "We're off."

CHAPTER TWENTY-SIX

Gone

With Dido at their side, Pandy, Alcie, Iole, and Homer walked quickly along the eastern road. At one point, they passed an insula and heard screams of pain coming from a room high above, piercing the morning quiet. Then the sounds of several slaps of a hand on what had to be bare skin.

"I am not getting any enjoyment from this, my little fish fillet," came Zeus's unmistakable voice.

Slap.

Scream.

"Now you know this is strictly for your own good," Jupiter's voice carried onto the road below.

Slap.

Scream.

All of a sudden, Hera and Juno's brilliant red behinds, complete with handprints, flashed in the window as they both tried to escape their joint monumental spanking.

"Oooooooh," said Pandy, with a laugh.

"Thank you, I won't be eating for days!" Alcie cried.

"Immortal posteriors," said Iole thoughtfully. "I don't know many humans who can say they've seen those."

"And lived," agreed Homer.

"Hera's just going to add it to the list," Pandy said, exiting the city proper and heading out onto the open road. " 'You saw my butt, now I really have to kill you!' "

"You saw her butt?" came a voice from under a nearby tree.

Everyone halted.

"Sounds like something that might be interesting. But upon further reflection . . ."

"Crispus!" Iole cried, flinging herself into his arms.

"Leaving without me?" he said, hugging her tightly.

"Our little girl is growing up," Alcie whispered to Pandy.

"Flying the nest," Pandy said, with a grin.

"I didn't know where you were to say good-bye," Iole said.

"Why good-bye?" Crispus said. "Why can't I come with you?"

Iole looked at Pandy, Alcie, and Homer. No one said a word; Crispus had proved himself beyond useful and very trustworthy.

"I have gold," Crispus said, producing a bag full of the aureus. "Okay, yes, I stole this if you want to get technical about it, but I *can* pay my way."

"You can pay for all of us," said Homer.

"I say yes," Pandy said.

"Works for me," Alcie agreed, nodding.

"Then it's settled," Crispus said, moving to relieve Iole of the burden of her pouch.

"And I say no," Iole said.

Crispus's face nearly fell onto the road, but before he had another chance to protest, Iole held her finger to his lips.

"Crispus, you should know that I simply adore you, and I don't care who hears it," she said, glancing at Alcie. "But . . ."

"But what?" he said.

"You're six."

And the horrible truth registered on everyone's face.

"At some point, either very soon or when we get to Greece," Iole went on, "Hermes will shift us once again into our correct time, and I'll stay the same, but you'll be six years old. As much as I want this to work, it never would."

Crispus said nothing for a long time, he only fought to keep his chin and his upper lip steady.

"You're not a Vestal anymore, right?" he asked finally, looking off into the distance.

"Correct."

"Then, when I am sixteen," he said, his voice low and steady, "you won't mind if I sail to Athens and seek you out, will you?"

"I'll be twenty-three, you *do* understand that?" Iole said, smiling.

"Understand it?" Crispus said, a grin breaking out. "I won't mind if you won't."

"Then I'll be waiting," said Iole, and everyone knew she'd be as good as her word. "Would you like the gold back?"

"No," Crispus said. "Keep it. Use it. Except, save a single coin for me when I see you."

"Thank you. I will."

Waving to Crispus until they crested a ridge and he disappeared from view, the four friends walked east for a bit, then changed direction and headed west when Iole casually mentioned that the Tyrrhenian Sea was a comparatively short walking distance away from Rome. A ship would be easy to find and, with any luck, Hera's bruised bottom would keep her preoccupied with exacting revenge upon her husband long enough not to bother with them as they sailed homeward, for the final time, to Greece.

GLOSSARY

Names, pronunciations, and further descriptions of gods, Demigods, other integral immortals, places, objects, terms, and fictional personages appearing within these pages. Definitions derived from three primary sources: Edith Hamilton's *Mythology: Timeless Tales of Gods and Heroes*; Webster's Online Dictionary, which derives many of its definitions from Wikipedia, the free encyclopedia (further sources are also indicated on this Web site); and the author's own brain.

entourage (ahn-TOOR-ahge): a group following or attending to some person (important or otherwise).

Iugula (eew-GEW-la): a Latin term meaning "kill him!"

Kraken (CRACK-en): a sea monster. Sometimes it resembles an island, sometimes an octopus. It is most commonly found in Scandinavian lore.

pollicem premere (POHL-issum PREE-murh): a Latin term translating to "to press the thumbs," which meant to spare a life.

proscription (pro-SKRIP-shun): the act of dooming to death or exile; a decree that prohibits or condemns something or someone.

taper (TAY-purr): a candle.

tempus fugit (TEM-puss FEW-jit): a Latin term meaning "time flees." In modern usage, this is more commonly translated as "time flies."

una malorum semper (OOOH-nah mal-OR-umm SEM-per): Latin for "one of the worst evils EVER."

ACKNOWLEDGMENTS

Thanks to Scott Hennesy, Stephanie Erb, Melanie Mohr, Sydney Cahill, and Caroline Abbey. As always, special thanks and love to Sara Schedeen.

DONALD AGNELLI

Carolyn Hennesy

is the author of all of Pandora's Mythic Misadventures, as well as the *New York Times* bestseller *The Secrets of Damian Spinelli*. As an actress, her work can be seen on both big and little screens (prime-time and daytime). In addition to her full-time acting and writing careers, Ms. Hennesy also teaches improvisational comedy, is an avid shopaholic, and studies the flying trapeze. She lives in the Los Angeles area with her fab husband, Donald, two cool cats, and two groovy dogs.

www.carolynhennesy.com

PANDORA
Gets Frightened

NEW YORK TIMES
BESTSELLING AUTHOR
Carolyn Hennesy

BLOOMSBURY

The flame at the end of the rope had grown much smaller—evidence that the air around them was becoming thick with death. Evidence that they were getting closer to the end of the path. Six more times Alcie had changed Homer's wrappings and six more times she, Pandy, and Iole had looked, with sinking hearts, at the wound. Even though Pandy had cauterized the flesh surrounding the gaping hole, even though they had tried to keep it clean and covered; certain sections were now black, as if the flesh was dying ("rotting away," Pandy remembered from the first question of the gate-keeping ear), and other sections were oozing a greenish-white gooey substance. Dido had stopped licking days earlier and no one blamed him. No one had said a word to Homer, but he knew something was terribly wrong; he'd resisted the urge to touch his cheek to find out for himself how bad it was. Over the last two days, he'd grown silent and pensive; even Alcie knew better than to try to jolly him out of his depression and pain. Then, somewhere in the middle of their ninth day walking, Iole's legs simply gave out. Walking beside Pandy, she groaned as her legs buckled from underneath her. She sat in the middle of the path and started crying.

"I can't take another step," she sobbed, laying her head on Dido as he sat next to her. "I'm so sorry, Pandy. My legs . . . they're numb. Can't we just rest for a moment?"

Pandy was about to sit down next to Iole and give her a big hug. Once again, Pandy realized how much her friends were sacrificing, how much was being asked of them, and how great their efforts were—and all to help her. Before she could sit, however, Homer swiftly scooped Iole up and onto his shoulders. That single act of selflessness, knowing he was already in agony, made Alcie weep, which in turn made Pandy cry. At last, Dido began to howl. They continued along the path—the only one not bawling was Homer.

Then—only a short time later and without any warning—the flame flared up, growing twice as bright as it had been, as a very soft breeze blew across their faces and they heard the unmistakable sound of rushing water. Up ahead, the blackness was pierced by a dim light.

They emerged from between the rock walls of the path and out onto a long, shallow beach bordered by a flowing river. It *did* seem as if there were a sky over-head; Pandy could swear she saw the faintest hint of clouds against the night. She knew they were thousands of meters underground, yet the terrain was the same as it was topside: rocks, a river, scrubby bushes, a beach, cliffs—only completely lacking color. On the opposite shore, they saw a huge, black wall with an enormous gate lit by four blazing sconces, each one as big as Sisyphus's stone.

"Rope," Pandy said, as Homer set Iole on the ground, "thank you for your service. No more flame."

The rope extinguished itself without even a puff of smoke, and Pandy tucked it neatly away in her carrying pouch.

"Ah, I remember this all so fondly. Not!" Alcie said, then she pointed to a rather rocky section of the beach. "Right over there—that pile of rocks? That's where I regained *el conscioso* right after Hera killed me. Hey, where's Cap'n Charon?"

"Look!" Iole said, pointing.

Farther up, they all saw two other mighty rivers flowing into the one that lay before them.

"One is the Acheron, the river of woe," said Iole, almost reverently. "And the other is the Cocytus, the river of lamentation."

"Did *not* know that when I was here before, but then, I was having too much fun. Fun, fun times," said Alcie sarcastically. "Where's Charon? Where's the boat bully, I wanna know."

"And this . . . this is the Styx," Iole said in awe, looking at the flowing water only three meters away. "Pandy—it's the *Styx*. We've seen some amazing things—but this! Into this river Thetis dipped her son, Achilles—whom you will all remember *I* helped her to name—to make him invulnerable; holding him by his heel so that *that* was the only place on his body where he could be killed. The Styx is *that* powerful. This is the river of unbreakable oath by which the gods themselves swear! If Zeus himself made a promise and swore by this river, even he couldn't break it no matter what it was."

"Well," Pandy sighed, "he didn't. Not to me, anyway. All right, those are the gates to Hades. And they're wide open, just as Sisyphus said. Now how do we get across?"

"Where's Charon?" Alcie said, scanning the river. "He's not here, he's not on the river, and his boat's gone."

"Maybe he escaped?" asked Homer.

"Don't think so," Pandy said. "We didn't meet anyone else on the path. The dead just get 'sent' here, but humans and any spirit who leaves—like Eurydice—have to take the path. I think."

"Most times, you bet," said Alcie, remembering how, when she'd left the underworld before, Hades had actually materialized her into a tree in Baghdad.

"And speaking of the dead, where are they?" Iole asked.

"Huh?" Alcie started.

"This shore, according to every legend I've ever studied, is always crowded with the dead, waiting to be ferried across. There are stories that say some spirits, those who weren't buried properly with coins on their eyes to pay Charon, or those with not enough of a payment, are forced to wander this beach for eternity. But I see no one."

"Iole's right, Pandy," Alcie said. "I don't see dead people."

"That's because they're all out there," Pandy answered.

Alcie, Iole, and Homer followed her gaze.

Even in the pale light of the sconces, they could now see that the Styx was full of various shades and transparent forms; some swimming, some floating—all trying for the far shore. Pandy saw a few shades actually drag themselves out of the water, but as they watched, it became clear that the current was too much for most, and hundreds of spirits were being towed underwater and downriver—wherever it went.

All of a sudden, Alcie's arm shot out.

"There!" she cried. "Charon!"

Alcie was pointing toward an impossibly thin man stomping about at the water's edge on the opposite beach. His boat was nowhere to be seen, but he still had ahold of the long pole he used to steer, push, and pull the ferry across the river. At the moment, he was trying to drive the dead who'd managed to get across the Styx back into the river if they didn't have the proper payment.

"Oh, yeah, you deranged old hydra," Alcie said acidly. "I'd know you anywhere. *That's* how he treated *me* until I bopped him one."

As Homer and the girls watched, one spirit, on the verge of dragging itself out of the water while being poked with the pole, grabbed the other end and forcefully pulled a very surprised Charon back into the Styx. The spirit, after standing on the shore, conked Charon on the head with his very pole—then tossed it into the river, where it got caught in the shallows.

"Score one for the dead guy!" Alcie said with a whoop.

"We still have a problem," Pandy said.

"How do we get across?" said Iole, finishing Pandy's thought.

"Same as them," Homer said. "Come on."

As he headed toward the water's edge, Alcie caught him.

"Hang on, handsome."

"Homer, this is the Styx and we don't know what could . . . ," Iole began.

"I get it, Iole. Okay? I do," he said, cutting her off. "But while you all have been watching the ferryman, I have been assessing the options. That's what I trained—for a few moons, anyway—in gladiator school to do when faced with a no-win situation. Here, there's only one way. There's no boat and no bridge. The water's not hurting the spirits, and we have no choice."

Pandy looked at Alcie and Iole. After a moment, she shrugged.

"When Homer's right, he's right."

"Just try to keep your head above water," he cautioned. "Y'know, just in case. And don't drink any of it."

"As if!" said Alcie.

Pandy went to step into the river first, but Homer gently pulled her back.

"I'm leading this," he said forcefully. "Iole, you're behind me, then Pandy and Alcie will bring up the rear. She's just a little stronger than you, Pandy, and we need our anchors on each end. Everyone, hold hands."

Homer stepped into the mighty Styx and everyone immediately looked at his face to see if there was a change—any pain—anything.

"It's fine," he announced. "A little warm actually. Stay against me if you can; I'll try to block the current . . . and the bodies."

"Dido, come!" Pandy called as Dido began to bark, running to the water's edge and then backing off.

"Oh, he's not liking this one bit," Pandy said. "Come on, boy. Follow us."

All at once, Dido's gaze became focused intently on the river—at least that's what Pandy thought; she couldn't really see his irises in the dim light. It was as if he was calculating something very tricky.

"What's he . . . ?" Alcie began.

Then, without warning, Dido ran headlong toward the river. But instead of landing in the water, each paw landed on top of a spirit body floating by. Dido raced across the Styx as if he were following a path of stepping stones, making certain to lift his paw off before the spirit went underwater. Within moments, he was on the opposite shore, barking triumphantly.

"Youths and maidens," Pandy said when she could talk again after being stunned into silence, "I give you— my dog!"

"What a performance!" Alcie crowed. "He could do two shows a night with Wang Chun Lo."

"Okay," Homer said. "He can do it, we can do it."

They waded out into the flowing water—it was warm, very warm—and found they could stand. At its deepest point, Pandy could just touch the river bottom with her big toe. Halfway across, Iole thought she had a firm footing on a rock, but her foot slipped on the slimy surface, and her head went under.

"Iole!" Pandy cried as she and Homer lifted Iole's head out of the water. "Did you swallow any of it?"

Iole blinked and shook her head.

"I'm fine!" She smiled. "Moving on!"

Pandy smiled back—but in that moment, she noticed that the firelight from the sconces stopped glinting off of Iole's hair. Iole's long black hair was now fully soaked—and dull; as if someone had coated it with cold sheep's fat. They were nearly on the opposite shore when she felt Alcie go under—then pop back up.

"Here!" Alcie said. "I'm right here."

Finally, Homer stepped up and onto the riverbank and hauled Iole next to him. Pandy found her own footing, then crawled the rest of the way onto the soft dirt as Homer lifted Alcie up and out of the Styx with one arm. After only a moment, Pandy got to her feet. She looked at the forbidding black gates, tall and seemingly covered in a dark pitch—and open.

"Okay," she said, turning back to her friends. "No time to lose. It looks like . . ."

Then her voice faltered.

Alcie's eyes were huge and Homer's mouth was agape. They were staring at her with the same look, she was certain, of shock and disbelief that was on her own face as she looked at them.

Alcie's skin from face to toe was the color and shine of copper. Her reddish hair now actually *was* copper, the curls and waves made of a thin copper wire. Homer's hair was still blond, but his skin had taken on a blackish-blue sheen—as if he was covered in iron.

Pandy looked at her own hands, arms and legs; they were a deep, rich bronze that glinted in the firelight. It was only after they realized that each of them was shining like metal did they look at . . .

Iole.

She wasn't standing slack-jawed, as they were. She wasn't examining every inch of her skin as they'd begun to do; she didn't even register surprise. She looked from one to the next, her eyes rather vacant and her skin dull. Iole definitely wasn't shining. In fact, she looked like she'd been covered in gray chalk.

"What in the underworld happened to us?" Alcie said, looking at the fine copper hairs coming out of her forearm.

Without thinking, Pandy looked at Iole, who she knew would have some sort of answer. But Iole just gazed back at Pandy as if the question hadn't even been asked. To her amazement, Pandy didn't panic; she just began to deduce.

"It's the Styx," she said. "It has to be. We went in, we were fine. We came out and . . . this."

"Like Achilles," said Homer.

"Exactly!" said Alcie.

"But not exactly," Pandy countered. "His mother, Thetis, just held him by the ankle and dipped him in for, like, a second. That's what made him invulnerable everywhere but his heel. But we were in there for . . . what?"

"A lot longer," said Iole.

"Arrows would bounce off Achilles like his skin were made of metal," said Homer.

" 'Like' it were metal," Pandy said. "Only our skin *is* metal! Great Zeus, I'm *bronze*!"

"But I can still pinch my flesh," Alcie said, grabbing the skin between her thumb and forefinger.

"Then it must mean we only have some sort of metal coating," Pandy answered.

"Is it going to make us sick? Will it ever come off?" Alcie asked. "Are we going to stiffen up like boards? Are we gonna die?"

"Alcie, calm down," Pandy said. "If it didn't hurt Achilles, I don't think it's gonna hurt us. Besides, there's nothing we can do about it right now."

"Why isn't anyone else affected?" Homer asked, looking at the spirit bodies floating in the Styx.

Before anyone else could think of an answer, Iole shuffled her feet.

"They're dead. We're not."

Calling all modern goddesses!

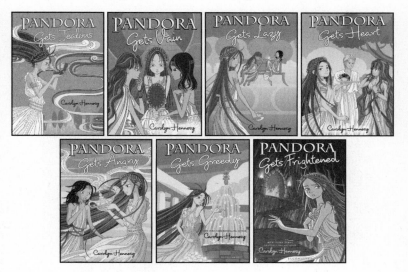

Don't miss Pandora's adventures as she and her BFFs try to collect the seven evils before Pandy becomes the most unpopular maiden in Athens . . . *and* goes down in history as the girl who ruined the world.

www.pandyinc.com

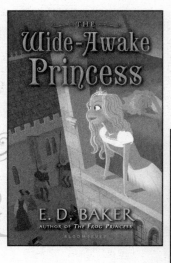